[INSIDE BACK COVER]

SEVEN CONTROLLED VOCABULARIES

2004

[AIRPORT NOVEL MUSICAL POEM PAINTING THEORY FILM PHOTO LANDSCAPE]

: TAN LIN

FOREWORD
LAURA RIDING
JACKSON

LIMITED AVAILABILITY:

YALE YOUNGER
WAL-MART
ASCII
PSA
S

LIBRARY OF CONGRESS CATALOGING-IN-PUBLICATION DATA

LIN, TAN, 1957-

SEVEN CONTROLLED VOCABULARIES AND OBITUARY 2004, THE JOY OF COOKING :
AIRPORT NOVEL MUSICAL POEM PAINTING FILM PHOTO HALLUCINATION LANDSCAPE /
TAN LIN.

    P. CM. — (WESLEYAN POETRY)

    ISBN 978-0-8195-6928-8 (CLOTH : ALK. PAPER) — ISBN 978-0-8195-6929-5 (PBK. :
ALK. PAPER)

    I. TITLE.

    PS3612.I516S48 2009

    811'.6—DC22

                    2009018192

PUBLISHED BY WESLEYAN UNIVERSITY PRESS

MIDDLETOWN, CT 06459

PRINTED IN THE UNITED STATES OF AMERICA

5   4   3   2   1

WESLEYAN UNIVERSITY PRESS IS A MEMBER OF THE GREEN PRESS INITIATIVE. THE
PAPER USED IN THIS BOOK MEETS THEIR MINIMUM REQUIREMENT FOR RECYCLED PAPER.

 THIS PROJECT IS SUPPORTED IN PART
BY AN AWARD FROM THE
NATIONAL ENDOWMENT FOR THE ARTS.

FOR/TO

11/07
2.21

The Joy of Co

king Tan Lin

SEVEN CONTROLLED VOCABULARIES

2004

THE JOY OF COOKING

[AIRPORT NOVEL MUSICAL POEM PAINTING FILM PHOTO LANDSCAPE]

: TAN LIN

WESLEYAN UNIVERSITY PRESS

MIDDLETOWN, CONNECTICUT

AND OBITUARY

FOREWORD
LAURA RIDING JACKSON

ACKNOWLEDGEMENTS

I wrote this book while I was a Post-doctoral Research Fellow at Liverpool John Moores University between 1999 and 2002, and I am very grateful to the Department of Literature and Cultural History, especially Pam Morris, for my appointment, without which the work would not have been possible. I would like to thank the following people for talking to me about the ideas and for reading drafts of the material: Matt Jordan, William Outhwaite, Charlotte Raven, Judith Williamson. I'd also like to thank Verso, and especially my editor Jane Hindle, for publishing the book. My family has been immensely supportive as always.

The illustrations on the following pages appear by courtesy of the copyright holders: p. 45: Stanley Spencer, *The Resurrection, Cookham* (1924–27). © Tate, London 2001. p. 237: Hieronymus Wierix, *Christ in the Wine Press (c. 1600)*. © Copyright The British Museum. p. 256: The *Guardian* newspaper front cover (*G2* supplement), 9 July 2001. Artwork by Daniel Hansen. Thanks to The Organisation and the *Guardian*. .

The photograph on p. 182 is by the author.

EDITORIAL NOTE

My collaborative aim in the production of this work has been to offer a series of intra-textual corrections in a typescript produced and renovated over several decades by more than one author. There are numerous errors of omission because blandness has no boundaries. Plagiarism is another manner. It was one of the necessary aims of revision.

Much of the work involved considerably less labor, was less meaningful in its aims, being merely a mechanical transcription of a clear text, but in other places more idiosyncratic handwritten notations or stylistic devices, or even choices of words have made the production more difficult and less literary than it need to have been. Such work is of the past of course. Such reading is of the present.

There is nothing that can come between between indifference and a form of redun-dancy. Except perhaps an omission. Multiple authorial redundancies could not be avoided. These lapses were welcomed wherever they might have been found in the text. Accordingly, there is nothing spectral, bracketed [   ] or metaphysical that remains, which is merely the husk of things that were true at the moment when they were once, [hallucinated] and by once I mean once written down without hope for any future, imagined or otherwise intended. There is truth and there is truth.

New York, 2004

编者的话在这项工作的生产我的合作目的，是要提供一系列的intratextual更正在打字生产，几十年整修由一个以上的作者。有很多的遗漏错误，因为枯燥无味是没有边界的。抄袭是另一种方式。它是必要的修订目标之一。大部分工作涉及的少得多的劳动，是有意义的减少其目的，这种说法仅仅是一个明文机械转录，但在其他地方更奇特手写的批注，或文体设备，甚至有选择的话使生产更加困难，少文学比须获。这些工作是当然的过去。这种阅读是本。没有什么能与冷漠之间，和一个冗余的形式。或许除了遗漏。多作者的裁员是无法避免的。这些失误在任何地方受到了欢迎，可能已经在文本中找到的。因此，没有什么谱，方括号[]或形而上学的，剩下的仅仅是事物的皮那些目前真正当他们一次，我的意思是由一次一次写下没有任何未来的希望，想象或试图。有真理，有真理。 2004年，纽约

A Field Guide to American Painting

ES

13 plates

Laura Riding, *Anarchism Is Not Enough*

What are the forms of non-reading and what are the non-forms a reading might take? Poetry = wallpaper. Novel = design object. Text as ambient soundtrack? Dew-champ wanted to create works of art that were non-retinal. It would be nice to create works of literature that didn't have to be read but could be looked at, like placemats. The most exasperating thing at a poetry reading is always the sound of a poet reading.

PLATE 1

FW HW 1¼" − 1"

What [   ] you are seeing is executed in Director and plays independently of any
intuited reading [voice] practices. It takes place in real time, and like a feedback loop
it is different each time it is played. The work was executed in b/w because b/w is
more soothing than color. Halfway through the program, a color randomizer has been
inserted to provide a greater sense of visual permutation, change and pleasure. One
word, then another, and finally a third follow each other in a kind of slow-motion,
time-lapse photography.

[S]

PLATE 2

SIDE B

Poems to be looked at vs. poems to be read vs. paintings to be sequenced vs. paintings to be sampled. Everything that is beautiful is a code for something that is already known. Nothing should be unknown. The program [   ] code you are watching generates 16.7 million different shades of color backgrounds. Some of these are suggestive. None of them functions in place of memory. Memory cannot be sequenced. Memory is usually non-designed. You are about to enter:] Three rooms. Mirror balls. Roving wallpaper. Disco. Home Furnishings. Lifestyle. Getting up [   ] and having a drink.

PLATE 3

C

Of course, in some novelistic vein, sequencing is highly absorptive, and so at the subliminal, i.e., non-designed level, the sequencing allows reading itself to become abstract, [bracketed] hypnotic, and [mesmerizing.] The problem with most poetry, like most design and architecture, is that it is a little too bourgeois. For this reason, the poem [or novel] should never be turned off. It is unfortunate but everyone says "cogito" in the Franco-American novel. Like a thermostat, it should regulate the room's energies. This allows the piece to constantly erase itself. As we all know, poetry and the novel should aspire not to the condition of music but to the condition of relaxation and yoga. A lot of people think great poems should be memorized. As anyone who has ever read a painting will tell you [like Ed Ruscha], paintings, like poems, are most beautiful [and least egotistical] at the exact moment in which they are forgotten, like disco and other Four on the Floor Productions.

PLATE 4

Each sequence or sentence, i.e., word set, runs 7.2 seconds or the amount of time it takes to pronounce each word, one word at a time. 7 is generally thought to be the number of things the human brain can readily remember. George Miller did pioneering studies on this and his theory is called Miller's Number Seven. Hence, most phone numbers are seven digits in length. 7.2 seconds is hopefully just long enough to get the reader/viewer into a groove. It might suggest a strobe light going off at timed intervals. The interval can be beautiful because the interval can be dubbed. Relaxation like non-designed home décor, has no real bounds. It supplements that thing known as real life. That is why it is so pleasurable to read.

Someone (I think) said the time for poems written with words and the era of reading poems with feelings in them is long gone. Today, no poem should be written to be read and the best form of poetry would make all our feelings disappear the moment we were having them. This sequencing of "events" constitutes a code more uncrackable and soothing than anything we could actually see. "Paintings to be read" → "poems to be looked at." A beautiful poem should rewrite itself one half-word at a time, in predetermined intervals. With their numerous circuit boards, televisions and computers do this; together, they enhance the microproduction and sequencing of feelings heretofore thought inaccessible, complex, or purely entropic. If all paintings could just be codes projected onto a wall, those names (accessories) for things canceling the wall would be more beautiful than anything we could feel.

取消的牆是更美好的東西，我們可以感覺到。

PLATE 5

25

Right, left.
Top, bottom.

Nothing that is negative is simple. Everything that is artificial is related to everything else in the room. Poetry should aspire to the most synthetic forms (the colors or numbers around it) and the most synthetic forms are to be found in houses with rectilinear walls, hallways, and foyers. Each wall separates one space from another. Everything that can be divided is divided into its proper sequence (i.e. style) of ones and twos. Private spaces are over-elaborated and under-inhabited. Public spaces are under-elaborated and lack sufficient feedback. Things that are living vs. things that are dead vs. languor.

For this reason, poetry (like a beautiful painting) ought to be replaced by the walls that surround it and doors that lead into empty rooms, kitchens and hypnosis. A poem should be camouflaged into the feelings that the room is having, like drapes, silverware, or candlesticks. All painting should aspire to the condition of encyclopedias, sequencing and b/w diagrams:

B SIDE

What are the forms of non-painting and what are the forms a non-painting might take? What are the non-forms of viewing and what are the forms non-looking might take? Painting as slow-motion film script? Canvas as ambient soundtrack? Dewchamp wanted to create works of art that were non-retinal. It would be nice to imagine a painting that didn't need to be looked at but could be sampled, like the newspaper, the television or the weather. A beautiful painting is a painting that disappears one half-brushstroke at a time. Like a thermostat, it should merely regulate the other colors and furniture in the room. Ad Reinhardt was wrong. Everything that is painted is sitting next to everything else that is not. The beautiful painting is involuntary. It should repeat itself endlessly in the background, like plants or a sofa. Only in this way can it repeat its own perceptual mistakes. As anyone who has ever sequenced a painting will tell you, perceptual mistakes are never sublime. A painting should expire just before we look at it, just like the drapes. The most annoying thing at an art museum is always the wall with a painting hanging on it.

PLATE 6

EA V1 m: 1nm: o

OVERLOADED GRID

S   M   M
R

PLATE 7

29

CLII . . . . No. 52,576 +

"NIAGARA FALLS IS JUST A KIND OF PAINT."

PLATE 8

What would it be like to look at a poem? It would be the most beautiful thing in the room that could stand to be looked at. It would be more beautiful than the thing itself. A beautiful poem is a poem that can be repeated over and over again. You are reading about a poem comprised of a thousand wayward looks. Look. A beautiful poem is a painting that can be repeated over and over again. Repetition is the only thing that makes something more perfect than it already is. For this reason, there is always a gaze that does not reach inside the face (I was looking at). That should be the gaze of poems that think they are paintings.

Andy Warhol understood this and he repeated the look of a painting every time he painted the same thing over and over and over and over. That is why he painted over the faces of photographs. Nothing is more beautiful than a face when it is repeated like (a word for) make-up. Novels were the earliest form of photography known to the human retina. That is why books are rarely mistaken for paintings. Paintings, unlike words, die the minute they attach themselves to a wall. Someone else said, "Excitement is the only thing in the world that cannot be predicted."

figure 1

figure 2

EAN 8/13

'NIAGARA FALLS IS JUST A KIND OF PAINT.'

INSERT PAGE 2^

'尼亞加拉瀑布只是一種塗料。

PLATE 9

78

My name is Dorothy. Because we like to come to a given space of our choosing, everything we see tends to look like a diagram or flowchart, as if it were designed to produce comfort zones, trance passages, or luck. Here is a house, here are its binary coordinates.

PLATE 10

H

I was reading a story about the anti-actress Chloë Sevigny, who is the most chased-
after fashion trendsetter now because she is "ugly-beautiful," wears "vintage prairie
dresses one day and Yves Saint Laurent the next," and seems negligent and muse-
like at the same time. She often claims not to know what she is wearing. She moves
around the room like an "anti-cheerleader." She goes shopping in Hello Kitty under-
wear. She played a vapory deb in *The Last Days of Disco* and, in *Boys Don't Cry,* a
trailer-park girl who falls in love with a boy who's really a cross-dressing girl. She can
make a beret look very recent. Her publicist announced: "She is trying to dissociate
herself from fashion at the moment." When I think of Chloë Sevigny, I feel the code-
book wobbling on my retina. Someone said: "Anticipation is an interesting and dif-
ficult thing to produce."

SOURCES
l.2 Bob Morris
l.5 Jorge Ramón

PLATE 11

+   −

The ultimate lifestyle exercise for a home is its television. It produces error after error.
If knowledge unlike pleasure takes place in a network, a painting should pursue itself
in a set interval of time, i.e., the time allotted to it. The ideal interval is programmed,
usually three or seven or twelve, and expands indefinitely. In that way all the words,
like portraiture or shades of color, could be replaced by something that reminded
one of a couplet, an integer, a television set, a phone number or the revolving sea-
sons. If one doesn't have a television set it is necessary to make one. It is now spring
or it is now autumn when you read this. The temperature is the same across all three
screens. Somewhere it is summer and I am losing someone because she is already
gone. The television set is sitting on the windowsill. It resembles a canvas. These
are the feelings television has and these are the ways we make our feelings disappear
into them, like small pieces of ice. The best paintings like poems make our feelings
evaporate at a constant rate like a disco, which is nothing but a rotating system of
words masquerading as numbers. I think it is snowing and I worry that the guests
will be late. I flick on the screens. This is an election year, of course. How to incite
the idea of reading without reading? How to accessorize reading as a practice similar
to entertaining? One comes and then one goes. One adds something and then one
subtracts something else.

The most precious commodity in modern life is time. I live in a house like a series
of loops, plus signs

+   =

PLATE 12

As any junkie will tell you, addiction knows no cause and occurs without memory. The best paintings, like words, expire like photographs of themselves. As such, the space for paintings and for experiencing paintings ought to take place backwards and as if they were erasing themselves

➔ *c*

paintings like words can be read as an equation for any number of diagrammatic surfaces: inexactitude, thought, the false arc of the historical. All paintings should be flowcharts of paintings and inhabit a decorated space. A painting like a poem is just a space that is showing up somewhere else. It should be ahistorical and undesigned and as homogeneous as possible. Like a book, it should aspire to the most taciturn forms of expression such as greeting cards, photographs of outer space, video monitors turned off, slightly incandescent lightbulbs, automobile windshields at night, billboards, cheap but glossy high-quality reproductions (of photos or paintings), banners, escalators, central air-conditioning, airports, ticket stubs, sheetrock, flags. You are looking at a book. Look at what is reflected: symbols that pass before it before they become emotions. In paintings, all emotions become the symbols of things that they are not.

Like the Pantone color chart, the beautiful book is a diagram of "historical inexactitude" which reflects (by turning) something "not there." A very beautiful painting should have its pages turned endlessly and without thought. What is "not there" is opposed to what appears in a poem or building or painting. It should never be necessary to turn a page when reading.

The page should turn before you got there. This is known as history.

PLATE 13

A Field Guide to The American Landscape

(8 plates)

PLATE 1

E

PLATE 1 Lumens. Clay. A grove. What does it mean when the world forgets the things that are repeating themselves beside it? Like a photograph, I believe everything that was once imaginary takes place on a surface that is real and cannot be repeated. Every novel should, like a chain of chemical reactions or code, be photographed or painted as a series of E's, a grid, a box, or lines. Only in that way do the memories we are not having become visible, somewhere to the left of what we were anticipating.

surface.

a diagram of a golf course

(drawing a)

(nostalgia)

PLATE 2

LECTURE (Panel 77/60)

FLIRT (#3522 RED)

PLATE 3

A

Instead of a photograph, A, that merely repeats something, a souvenir or keepsake, I wanted this to resemble nothing but itself, and thus to capture the blankness and non-theatrical spaces of the world "out there." The least repetitive photographs are the photographs that make us forget the things that we love. That is why most landscapes are so boring to look at. A beautiful landscape is like a beautiful photograph is like a beautiful landscape is like a beautiful photograph. Such photographs erase people, relatives, household objects, other photographs, and landscapes at a steady velocity. That is why it is normally so difficult to fall in love with the same person twice.

Because each of these flowers, in April, may be counted more than once, the photograph seems to repeat itself endlessly, just like our feelings do. That is why photographs of landscapes or people or nature are usually meaningless. Such a photograph becomes a kind of definition of the theatricality of the world. If the world is a landscape, then our emotions become a reversed and private spectacle of all the things we cannot remember.

Yet everything about our desires is central to a point of fault. For this reason, the empty page corresponds to a location. If my eyes were like a newspaper, the photographs appear to revolve around the words like a series of imaginary facts, and then appear to double.

B

In any given landscape, B, like this, whatever is written down is beset by resemblances and whatever I hear I write down. No writing should ever be done while one is thinking about something. The newspaper on the other hand is purely temporal. It records phenomena as if they had just happened. If I have no memories of this (i.e., Plate 6), I consider this to have been the object of a desire or something that is reconstructed many years after the fact.

When I look at a landscape in a novel all I see is something that I have not had the time to forget. One waits patiently for the things that have happened already. In this landscape, something I forgot (once) is about to reverse itself and become exactly what it is. You can remember someone many times but you can forget them only once.

On the front page of today's *New York Times*, which I confuse with a landscape, in front of the flag, there is a photograph of an unspecified Federal building.

PLATE 4

My girlfriend thinks the world is constantly taking its own picture and walking away from it.

PLATE 5

Miyuke kissed me (autism)

like too many typos (impropriety)

(ym) in the background

PLATE 6

and not much later (11:51), out pops a pencil. My body is warmish. I feel stale. I have lost my job but not my teeth because it is Thursday. I have stopped watching this film, in fact I cannot stand the cinema because nothing could be more empty than the day it took place.

January 17   tab   eclipse

superflat   ghost-like   Jesus

PLATE 7

The cover of issue 3 showed a

"Russian sailor" with the caption

hair

PLATE 8

The caption read 25 silhouettes.

American Architecture Meta Data
Containers

(17)

NO 1

AWE BUILDINGS = READING MACHINES

What are the forms of American Written English [AWE] but a series of spaces we might not have inhabited had we lived less [coercive lives], eaten more organic vegetables or taken Xanax at night before retiring? The [words] like the buildings of our era are utterly indiscriminate and by indiscriminate I mean already forgotten. Like us they have been reflected back to us by other more efficient modes of relaxation such as the shopping mall, the television, abandoned lots, landscapes that have been photographed, interactive e-billboards, backs of books, the disco, electronic signatures, and fast food. All labeling schemes shall be as non-descriptive as possible.

2B 4H

The forms of our quietude are various and quotidian. Ever since she got married

(11/7/03)

my ex-girlfriend likes to listen to Wagner and the Mekons. Today [tomorrow] the things we do or do not read are just an accessory for the various things that connect us to our lifestyles. Nothing w/o a label can be valuable. A fountain like a book is an index of its own expiration. Nothing w/o a date can be forgotten. In the future, all buildings shall function as product logos and instructional diagrams.

[architecture and hygiene]
ADAM KALKIN

$27.95
Can. $43.95

UNIVERSE

GIS

What is the opposite of truth? Imagine yourself reading. Then imagine reading backwards so that nothing is variable (e.g., Douglas Huebler, *Variable Piece No. 5*) or allowed to move forwards. Reading is the most pleasing of surfaces and no text shall be designed to please. Every panel is a shortcut to the things it has just passed. Information = decoration. Like a swimmer caught in the butterfly stroke, movement takes place in multiple directions. The page is a quadrant filled with various codes that resemble flags. A man is drowning. A woman is sighing. A pet is taken out for a walk. In the fourth quadrant, which is usually left blank, no thing emotional shall be set in motion by random memory, or mirror emotions which appear to be un-moving.

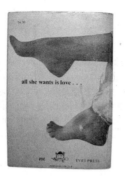

PRADA

Like our various selves, literature should function as a pattern with a label on it, like
the lines in a parking lot at the local A&P or the indistinguishable, partially imagined
street names found in private, gated communities throughout North America: Elm
Place, Elm Tree Lane, Ellingham, Elsingham, Ellen Tree Road, Elmwood Ave., Elm
Circle Rd., etc. The most beautiful books are the most invisible ones, just as a pink
chemise with embroidered flowers by Marc Jacobs would be almost meaningless
without a label and just as a Prada shoe should carry a red stripe down its sole or
a bag by Louis Vuitton should have its initials prominently scrambled all over its
surface *in order to* be read. And by read I mean not read in any meaningful way.
After all, who has really read a bag by Louis Vuitton or a sweater with a deliberately
unraveled collar by Martin Margiela although I have read these things for many
hours of the afternoon?

16 BIT

It is important never to design a recognizable text, just as it is better to never design a building or item of furniture. It would be better to merely skim these items at the point where they blur in relation to their multiple users or focal points. This is known as repetition. Speaking with one's lips creates the most delicate forms of local reading and diagrams of white noise that take the form of color, i.e., a delay. It would be useful to finally compile a dictionary of the various forms of delay that are possible. Delay for sunlight falling in trees. Delay for cigarettes. Delay for the sake of lovemaking. Delay for unidentifiable birdsong. And finally, the most difficult delay: delay for seeing itself. Between color and b/w, symmetrical rooms are located in asymmetrical space. All reading experiences are symmetrical and unbroken by words.

ACTUAL USE

As the mathematician Hermann Weyl noted: "A thing is symmetrical if there is something that you can do to it so that after you have finished doing it, it looks the same as it did before." Reading, unlike writing, should be like that.

LOGO

For this reason, the most powerful texts function like logos, a code wherein words
and reading are synthesized into looking and staring, i.e., they become primitive and
unmoving structures for the channeling of static information. As such they can
be read as styleless or exemplars of a *fonctionnalité absent*. Such texts aspire to the
furniture-like logos of multinational corporations, particularly gas and bank logos,
which can typically be read bidirectionally or rotationally. In their L→ R and R→ L
orientation, these circular logos mirror interior and exterior spaces. For this reason,
they are boring to read, and resemble things like parking tickets, ticket stubs, and
books like the Bible or *Dogs that Know When Their Owners are Coming Home*. A
logo-like text is text and reading instructions as one, and thus transforms the activity
of reading into a mechanical and premonitory activity wherein things that are read
become endlessly static and recognizable. Reading is nothing more than a pattern,
one that is not designed, where symmetry and asymmetry are indistinguishable.
Such readers act like open-source codes. Examples of open-source reading codes
include logos, flags, headlines, product labels, vibrating or hot colors, diagrams,
Muzak, things that are blurred, and neon language. These languages eschew the tra-
ditional book's desire to discover symmetry in the world beyond the book. No book
shall have a posthumous fame.

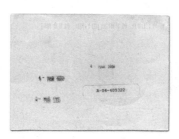

PREFACE to a DEPT STORE

I was at the Macy's on 34th and Seventh Avenue last month, at exactly 3:47pm on June 2, 2003. I had received an SMS that morning requesting me to assemble there, in the secured lobby area just inside the revolving doors at the Broadway and 34th Street entrance. Once there I was given a thin blue sheet of paper measuring 3x5 inches. On it was hand typed a message:

```
DIRECTIONS FOR USE:  ! EXCHANGE IMMEDIATELY !
1 dollar bill with someone,
drop the dollar bill
on the floor and then
leave as quietly as possible.
```

What is the "movement of an anecdote" but a blurry exit through a diagram of some missed opportunity? The performance produced 38 U.S. dollars, 4 HK dollars, and 2 Euros. Someone with a stopwatch timed the event at 47 seconds. Outside in the dispersing crowd I met [a woman] who would later become my girlfriend and later my wife. Her name was Clare [Churchouse] at the time. In Singapore at the Golden Locket Hotel, exactly the same thing was happening 6 months and one hour later. As I left the airport and later the hotel lobby and Macy's one month later, I kept thinking I was watching a painting or a movie theatre at the moment it started becoming something else. I have tried to remember this incident many times but the same image constantly assails me and I am no longer able to remember the date/time of the event or the age/size of my girlfriend/wife. I realize now that I have met her many times at many similar moments. Who is she? What is she doing at the moment I see her face? She is turning away and telling me that my project is "flawed." My wife's *Manhattan Diary* for 2/21/01 reads: "met author at Bulgarian Bar on Canal Street." She wrote that after the fact. This book is dedicated to her in that crowd where I do not see her. We were married on November 7, 2002, at City Hall in New York City.

Like shopping malls and other enclosures, consciousness is merely a generic mode of duration or thinking "without preconditions." Like everything else, consciousness is in need of micro-branding and rehearsal. Enjoyment is one of the most difficult emotions to predict, and the ideal movie or building or poem should be extremely predictable and convey as little information as possible. The kind of group thinking that takes place when shopping, voting or reading lacks functionality. In the informal, non-mob sequence at Macy's, a purposeless film within a film within a department store, the population center is micro-branded and meaninglessly re-enacted [one of the forms of convergence] in order to be dispersed or delivered like a logo. The logo is an anonymous murmur. MF said that.

We believe expenditure takes place without meaningful exchange, or we get repetitive gestures without significance. Airports, shopping malls, and golf courses are the most pleasing, crisis-free, and logo-ized of landscapes. They are mood-inducing delivery systems, schematas of unimposed identifications that make irrelevant the distinction between pre- and post-consumption. A golf course like a painting is consumed in almost the same way time and time again. That is why golf is so relaxing. Golf courses, cineplexes and shopping centers fringe population areas and function in the same way that pastoral poetry, the coffee house c. 1680, short bandwidth radio, or the only movie theatre in a small town once did. They remind us that we need to fall in love again and again and again with something that is unspecific, very repetitive, and very very general. The lights of the Varsity Movie Theatre in Athens, Ohio, where I grew up, reflect each night off the bricks of Court Street, but the marquee now reads Taco Bell, and the old balcony and stage are now the site of tables and the gentle, illumined prices of tacos and quesadillas. Our most beautiful emotions like a movie theatre or the pages of a Chinese cookbook or the price of 16 ounces of Pepsi are routine and anodyne. Either they existed before or they existed previously. All of our emotions vacation with incandescence as they dissolve.

"Architecture as Shelter with Decoration on It"

vs.

"Literature as Space with Language Attached to It."

Here is your **Moist Towelette**. It will clean and refresh your hands and face without soap and water. Self dries in seconds, leaving skin smooth and soft.

Directions: Tear open packet, unfold towelette and use.

 National
TOWELETTE CO.
Cinnaminson, NJ 08077
www.towelettes.com

MTR03 MADE IN USA   1   (856) 786-7300

"Architecture as Shelter with Decoration on It"

vs.

"Literature as Space with Language Attached to It."

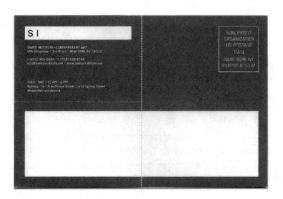

BOOKS That Function As BUILDINGS

AREA 51

Because certain books function as labels rather than mirrors, the most beautiful
things take place before our eyes for the most indignant of reasons. In them, reading
is beautiful because reading is generic and immaterial, like most of the buildings we
pass through [   ] and the streets we happen to be on. [As anyone] [who has
spent time on the Las Vegas strip] can tell you,

FUSE

there is minimal enclosure and negligent direction. Hence removing the jacket

➤

from a book is the best way to create a kind of empty enclosure within the book, or a
black box recorder or closed parking garage without it. One never really knows what is
beside a parking lot or a book. Such reading experiences aim for a uniformity in which
nothing is produced by the book's turning pages ← CVR

In such a bureaucracy of form, there is no plot and/or character. The page is spectral
[unformatted] and dumb. The book comprises a solid diagram, however illumined
[décor] by outside sources. Someone said Samuel Johnson, who was a great compiler
of things people have already said, *is* indignant and she was right but only in the
moment before she said it. The front of a book is always less interesting than the back
of a book.

Someone I love told me an anecdote is about the decline of something natural, like
the novel (insignia), a sports car or a t-shirt. A beautiful novel will give off anecdotes
at a relatively habitual rate. This is because a belief in anecdotes is like a belief in the
paranormal.

2,612,944

For this reason, any anecdote will tend to resemble things that are boring and a great
many other things will be more boring than any untold anecdote (of life), which is
completely un-repetitive and rarely generates anything good to read. As any reader
knows, no one has yet invented a novel that is capable of reading itself (sadism). That
is why novels today are so inconclusive and ill-formed: they resemble outlines of nov-
els we have already read, each with a troubling, hard core of meaning locked inside by
the author. As Gertrude Stein said resemblance is not repetition.

It would be nice if the book could be less spatially kinetic and more boring, like a mailbox with a name on it or a billboard. As anyone who has ever read a best-seller can tell you, reading experiences don't last very long and they tend to be as amorphous and formulaic as the individual human attention span will permit. Such a book would have the general effect of dispersing its community and converting all readers into non-readers. The reader of a book is irrelevant whereas the reader of an unread book is highly relevant as time passes and the reader goes elsewhere. Henri Bergson called disorder an order we cannot see. Similarly, the most beautiful poems suggest [   ] experiences that are highly inattentive and unwritten and the most beautiful [   ] are merely superficial indicators for other sorts of peripheral, coded, programmatic, functional or directional information that is applied to the surface of things like postcards, flat-panel displays, parking lots, brochures, street signs or other depthless objects. Hence the great interest early in the century in photographing landscapes [Geography] and inserting them into books, thus creating static monuments to Nature and/or its opposite: Culture.

| | III   IIII   IIIII

The ideal novel would not be necessary to read at all. It would have no inside or out-
side. All words would flow outwards like soft data. All "events" would be migratory
or reduced to background clutter. All novels would aspire to the condition of Muzak.
Production, dissemination and consumption would become one. All attention would
be leftover for an indeterminate amount of time. No one would fall asleep while read-
ing a book again. Aristotle was wrong. A novel like an event should not take place in
24 hours or less. Comprehension would cease to matter or would be deflected so
that all actions would seem to be taking place "somewhere else." Or not at all. Or
in slow motion. Or invisibly. Or against the grain of the visible. As everyone who has
ever watched a TV show about nature or wild animals mating can tell you, beauty like
reading lies in increasing forms of inexactitude. It is best to behave like an animal or
an insect when reading. In this way reading is more readily absorbed by the human
body. The most beautiful things in a novel are the things one didn't know one was
thinking about. For this reason, a novel should not tell a story of anything in particu-
lar. It should be an exercise in non-attention and non-development and the gradual
erasure of content. Of course all of this inexactitude, non-comprehension and non-
memory should all take place in time and be subject to duration rather than chronol-
ogy. Smaller fonts are more readily absorbed by the eye. I have never felt like an insect
except when I was in high school and I was asked to make a miniature pencil holder
in shop class.

KEY

time of day, nationality, v.
Muzak, start of color, division, an other side
freq., media, order, statehood, prelude to

MOLD
/✲✲#@+

Mold multiplies on existing structures where abortive mimicry takes the form of routine contrivance: carpets unrolled from shop entrances onto sidewalks, trash cans provided for customer convenience, ATMs installed in the front wall of a shop, banners, chained down sandwich boards, umbrellas, potted trees, public clocks, plastic flags on a string, Xmas lights, merchandise racks, menu boards, awnings. Mold, like airborne litter, feels redundant, spatially indifferent, and highly absorptive. As a mode of spatial indecisiveness, it spreads noise, flutter, and static in its path: shelf-talkers under vodka bottles, TV monitors above selling floors, fall-out litter in magazines, seasonal cardboard display stands in grocery store aisles, canned music, or even people—who work as greeters, survey takers, Ronald McDonald clowns, or seasonal Santa Clauses. Ironically, indoor Mold replicates Nature or items imported from peripheral geographies: as with survey takers and Santa Clauses mentioned above, but more obviously with engineered fake palm trees/flowers, fountains, vendors' carts, or the ubiquitous "park" benches found inside shopping malls. Similarly, outdoor Mold imitates man-made structures, as with the McDonalds on 42nd Street in New York, where the golden arches are replaced by a theatre marquee in order to blend in with the neighborhood. Mold is an oscillating parameter. The shopping mall is a suburban foliage "exchanged" for something it is not: a park enclosed by a street whose cars have been removed.

The oldest forms of seasonal Mold are the display windows in large department stores such as Saks Fifth Avenue and Marshall Fields, where panoramic display windows proxy for nature and even fluctuate, like real windows, with the seasons. Such windows are non-functional, i.e., they cannot be opened. Thus, the shopper's eye is mystified between looking in (at nature) at Christmas time and looking out (at culture) at other times of the year. Such greenhouse effects are paradoxically considered art rather than commerce. In places where browsing and tourism take place, advertisers and artists alike understand that mold in the form of serial images [photography in particular] impedes foot traffic and amplifies sales. Not surprisingly, Warhol dressed windows for Bonwit Teller. Earlier forms of mechanical mold were the flashing billboard or the slow-motion escalators in a department store, both of which retard time and create the delay that is the mirrored interior space of all commodities

Mies was wrong. Function erases form and makes it fuzzy. The era of [granular] architecture and finished buildings and destination shopping is past. In the coming century, the function of architecture and commodities shall be to destroy memory and historic places of interest at a standard rate and so disappear more completely into their surroundings. No buildings will need to be added to landmark registries. All landscapes like emotions will be pre-activated by the activity that has forgotten them. The same stretch of road on the way to the LAX or the CMH airport can last an hour or twenty minutes and is always approximate: we see exactly the same waste treatment plants, radio stations, Motel 6s, drive-ins, power grids, failed shopping malls, used car lots, freight yards, prisons, landfill architecture, playing fields, industrial elevators, public swimming pools, Quonset huts, tollbooths, storage facilities, research parks, and construction sites. As the suburb overtook outlying rural areas, it morphed into pastoral industrial "parks," lush corporate headquarters, and golf courses. The less a building resembles a building the more beautiful and banal it will be. The same is true of the landscape. It shall modulate into the more homogeneous and statistical spaces of our lives. Donald Judd was wrong. A building should be the most unspecific object imaginable. Our most beautiful desires are our most unspecific ones. What is the relation between moss on a building and a bar code?

insert photos

Does ACID Make a SOUND?

In the future shopping will signify increasingly efficient markets and the minimization in the valuation of goods and services. Various forms of non-branding techniques will become logos that advertise not companies but the materials (i.e., as information) themselves. Line extension will disappear. Composition/ingredient lists will become bar codes, which will in turn replace brand names. Shopping will begin to cater expressly to those who desire less or who do not desire at all, as opposed to the present system where desire and increased product variety go hand in hand. Advertising will become what it is already but in purer form: decreased information. In this scenario, shopping creates a utopian system of non-designed buying patterns wherein desire is minimized rather than maximized and in which the market erases itself and threatens to overwhelm the differences (supply and demand) that drive markets. Increasingly, goods and the information about those goods will come to mean one and the same thing. The difference is contracting.

You Appreciate Things of GREAT BEAUTY

I like to stare at things that cannot be read. Only in that way can the present be remembered. I need a menu to wash my car.

What is the relation between a fruit and a vegetable? A book transpires one letter and then one word at a time and nothing about reading can prevent this from happening. For this reason, books are best diluted or read over a good many years. Only things that are consumed endure beyond their shelf life. Nothing is really very different [if you say it] is. I had dinner yesterday at WD-50, which is a restaurant located where the new Fukienese area of Chinatown and the old pickle shops of the defunct Lower East Side almost come into alignment. The restaurant is at 50 Clinton Street and it has a post-Craftsman style décor with bulbous glass lamps that look like fluorescent flower bulbs. The chef's name is Wylie Dufresne. He is young and looks like a cowboy reincarnated as a skateboarder. His father Dewey is also a chef.

WD-50 is probably the only restaurant in Manhattan that makes you hallucinate the food you are eating while you are eating it. The food can be quite un-foodlike. I ate at the restaurant a few nights ago and afterwards my taste buds felt incongruous and ecstatic. I remember seeing something on another table that looked like dessert and I ordered it. A few moments later there were bonbon sized bits of pineapple on a plate. They had been soaked in something briny and had become pickles. Off to one side of the fruit was smeared what looked like hot fudge sauce except that it was made of ketchup and jalapeno peppers. The sauce was semi-frozen. The sauce was hot and cold and cold and hot I couldn't tell which. I put the pineapple in my mouth and it was like eating something that was once a vegetable. The chef had sprinkled some salt scented with what looked like dour chips of limes. It was not really necessary to eat the food; one could breathe it. When I put all this in my mouth I tasted so many things I forgot what was in my mouth. Eating at WD-50 is like reading Proust backwards. I looked over at a man at the table next to ours and he had the face of a six-year-old. The ideas of food erase the food itself and then become the food you did not think you were eating. Time passes inordinately or not at all. What is it like to eat an idea or its suggestion? As anyone who has eaten can tell you, the most beautiful memories are memories that one has forgotten how to have. Eating at WD-50 is like having psychoanalysis with a starch, a sugar, or a fat.

Uniforms. Prada. Books without authors.

NATURE Every era attempts to return to its version of the natural. In the 70s it
was air and nature. In the 80s it was discos and money. In the 90s it was the body,
nurtured by low fat food, which is valuable because it is ingested. In the 00s, it is
non-designed buildings, objects and food, all of which suggest a luxuriant return to
50s forms of standardization, reversed and applied to hyper-standard forms of buying.
Non-designed objects like staplers, waste baskets, juicers and toys for children now
appear to be the "things they are not." Reading a book should be like going out
to a restaurant or buying a candle holder. It should enhance the mood of the space
that it occupies. Shopping is *déclassé* because it is no longer a discrete activity but
has infused everything with its design.

C

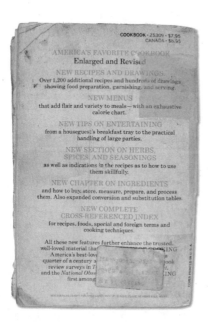

DISEASE Today most diseases are being transformed into lifestyles that can be modulated or modified. It is not uncommon for parents to give their children drugs (Zoloft, Paxil, and numerous other SSRIs) designed for adults, since such drugs don't cure illnesses but foster lightly regulated forms of mood alteration synonymous with parenting and growing up/old. In such a world all treatments, including drugs, are a domesticated, quasi-religious interface between self-diagnosis (self-consciousness) and its placebos—in our era, a host of naturalized treatments (acupuncture, herbal medicine, osteopathy, homeopathic cures, pyschoneuroimmunology, etc.). In the old days, "real" (synthetic) drugs eradicate disease from the somaform. Today "natural" drugs promote wellness, decentralize one's symptoms, and help one be oneself. In today's climate, diseases become less a form of medical non-fiction (hence the prevailing *mistrust* of physicians, the insurance industry and pharmaceutical companies) and more subjective, genealogical, spagyric, and ritual-like [poesis], as witness the over-the-counter treatments for depression such as the magical St. John's Wort, and the no-less-heavenly milk cures prescribed in the early twentieth century for such nosological nonentities as neurasthenia. Most pills today are deployed fictionally as non-fiction, i.e., color-coded lozenges, a kind of micro-information architecture [theatre calibrated as dosage] neatly packaged as an architectural escutcheon or fleur-de-lis, and reminiscent of the ornamental sugar icing and fondants on cakes and pastries. Pills are the new aphrodisiacs. Through them we prescribe the more diffuse patterning of our symptoms and our love lives.

FOOD   Modulo Check Character 1974

Restaurants of the future will be about the loss of ownership vis-à-vis one's place in the food chain. Accordingly, all choices will no longer be applicable. Menus will disappear. Computers will take individual orders and chefs will prepare all dishes to order. Everyone will eat something different, within reason. Dining out will be an extension of dining in. Eating out will begin to resemble smart information systems.

AN EVERGREEN BLACK CAT BOOK 🐱 $1.75
B-216

A LAYMAN'S GUIDE TO SOME SCENES
THE REVIEWERS LIKED BEST

(See page 1 inside for some reviewers' conflicting comments)

Printed in U.S.A.

95

HALLUCINATION

It is a well-known (fact) that textual (novelistic) operations of reading are rarely hallucinogenic or based on chance. Those that are are rare or vaguely indeterminate and hence only intermittently pleasurable. Those that are not are considered mawkish or experimental. These (rotating) intervals or surrounds of reading matter can be taken (imitatio) "of the lifestyles."

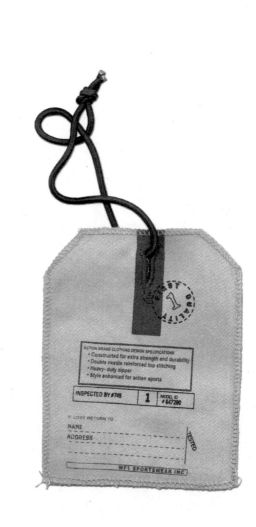

2 Identical Novels

Everything is a form of longing if you say it is. Nothing that is indignant is very ugly. Nothing that is not consumed exists for very long. T.S. Eliot said that. A friend of mine who likes to rip me off is an auto mechanic who was trained to repair Jaguars and Mercedes Benzes. They are the only cars he knows how to fix, and he has set up a shop called Foreign Motors in an old gas station where he works on cars, listens to Van Halen, and sleeps and lives as well. When my father passed away in 1989, I inherited my father's favorite car, a brown 1978 Mercedes SE. I had just moved to Charlottesville, Virginia, where I had been hired to teach literature. By the time I got the car, it leaked whenever I drove in the rain, and the floor absorbed all sorts of water from the road because the undercarriage was rusted out. I hardly ever drove the car because I always thought that it would rain, but for some reason I could never bring myself to sell it. And in that way I was never allowed to think about driving at all or experience my feelings of driving while I was driving but only after I came home or when I was no longer driving, which was the more relaxing part of driving anyway. Reading like consumption should be very fast and very hypnotic and very wasteful of the actual time of reading so that one doesn't really know what one is reading or consuming or throwing away at the moment one is throwing it away. I never knew why my father loved that car or why I kept it for so long. One should never know one is reading a book when one is reading it.

FISH BONES OR OTHER ACCIDENTAL BONES ARE TAKEN BETWEEN FINGER AND THUMB AND REMOVED BETWEEN COMPRESSED LIPS PITS AND SEEDS MUST BE EATEN QUITE BARE AND CLEAN IN THE MOUTH AND DROPPED INTO THE CUPPED FIST AND THEN ONTO THE PLATE THE PITS OF STEWED PRUNES OR CHERRIES THAT ARE EATEN WITH A SPOON ARE MADE AS CLEAN AS POSSIBLE IN THE MOUTH (WITH THE TONGUE AND TEETH) AND THEN DROPPED INTO THE SPOON WITH WHICH YOU ARE EATING AND CONVEYED TO THE EDGE OF THE PLATE BUT IT IS HORRID TO SEE ANYONE SPIT SKINS OR PITS INTO A SPOON OR INTO THE PLATE UNLESS REALLY DRY AND WITH LIPS COMPRESSED

212-477-2900

50 Clinton Street
New York NY 10002

1:1

Literature like everything else [monarchism, class distinctions, mercantilism, free markets] should just be a form of packaging, which is a method for extracting non-variable information at the moment before it is released. All information exists to be regulated (i.e., reversed) by the surface of a book. Hence the notion of copyrights, which are projections of a book's normal lifespan and which expire [U.S.] after the author's lifetime plus 75 years. In the world outside the west, it is understood that all reading practices shall be non-time-based and decorative. In that way they can be made ever more abstract and vague, like the non-illusionistic theatres of the east: Noh drama, Kathakali, Peking Opera. Such static forms are mechanical and thus are opaque and homogeneous to spectators lacking the decoding system. Generic information is perfect information. Most books, unfortunately, are very imperfect: that is why they are read more than once. The surface is simulated, i.e., restricted by its own surface reflections/variants or logos/editions. Visual flow disturbances (blurring, misreading, transposing) and other directional distortions are endemic on the surface, which is unable to fully contain them. All surfaces like books thus have a typical duration (T), which represents the time it takes to scan the book for false uncertainties. Reading a novel is like looking at a movie of a rainbow in order to get one's bearings.

[Schrodinger, E.]

1935 "The present situation in quantum mechanics" in *Naturwissenschaften*, **23**, pp. **823-828**.

All reading shall be fully warrantied or deregulated by fair use laws. A friend of mine, Tom Newlin, is an amateur farmer and professor of Russian. In **2001**, he wrote a book on the Russian graphomaniac Andrei [Timofeevich] Bolotov who is best known for writing three books in a single **24**-hour sitting, for writing the equivalent of **350** volumes of mostly unpublished work during his lifetime, and for writing an individual poem to every plant in his garden and when he ran out of plants, every non-plant in his house. Over the course of his life, he wrote "To Thee, O Grass Settee," a sonnet to Bolotov's favorite sod sofa (he had three), and "Verses to the Stand for my Pocket Watch." My friend Tom is actually the opposite of Bolotov. For Tom, getting two or three words down can take a week and so Tom is actually a reader of an altogether more diffident and cumbersome sort: he is the opposite of a graphomaniac, i.e., he is a very very slow serial reader. One might say his reading practices are highly residual, as if everything he was reading were a code or compressed object. To understand something he has to read it two or three times over the course of many months. Sometimes a reading, which is really the rehearsal for a reading, can transpire over years. Tom says he picked up this practice in childhood when he lived in a part of Philadelphia called Secane (pronounced SEE-CANE) and grew up on what was basically a farm enclosed by suburbs: **16** acres of dilapidated farm and unused pasture, with a number of animals, mainly cats, that were old and blind and incontinent. Because books were scarce and the cats would run in and out of the rooms with birds in their mouths, Tom would read books over and over again. It is a very beautiful experience when you read and read and read and read a book so slowly and methodically and recursively that all you do is keep waiting for something to repeat like a plant or an animal that comes into the room you are reading in. But of course a book never does come in like that, in the same way that your childhood never repeats childhood until you become an adult. As any child can tell you, you should never have to put down a book to read it. Everyone loves to see a plant become another plant or an animal become another animal. Nothing is slower or lovelier than a book that knows how to reproduce.

RFID

The first book Tom remembers having read, when he was seven, was a reprint [school edition] of Jules Verne's *Twenty Thousand Leagues Under the Sea*, and since 1977 he has amassed a collection of as many different editions of the book as he can find in used-book stores, Salvation Armys, thrift stores, and the like: Pocket Books, Magnum Easy Eyes, Fawcett Premiers, Signet Classics, Washington Square Paperbacks, Plumes, Mentors, Amazing Stories, Oxford World Classics, Everyman Editions, Serpent Books, Scholastics, a host of generic elementary-school editions sold through school book clubs, Norton Criticals, Dover Thrifts, Fantastic Stories, Penguins, Livres des Poches, Evergreens, Puffins, Pelicans, and Bantams. Every time he finds a new cover, he promptly goes home and speed-reads the book and he has now read *Twenty Thousand Leagues Under the Sea* 137 times, carelessly, and in six different languages, including Spanish, Russian, Korean, French, Chinese, and Greek. He even tried learning Arabic once to half get through a version he found in a pensione in Florence.

One evening after drinking, Tom confessed to me that he had never really bothered to think about the book at all in all his years of reading, and that he had not really ever experienced anything while reading the book except the books' numerous covers: one-eyed octopi, riveted nautiluses connected to leathery breathing tubes, a lead balloon that looks like a manhole cover, photosynthetic seaweed, farm-like fields of layered oceans and raisin-shaped islands, barnacled or tentacle-entwined periscopes, and even what looks like a large manatee on a book from Brazil. For Tom, the 1930s with its images of red-eyed sea monsters becomes the 1950s with its Soviet-style submarines becomes the 1960s with its long-haired sea creatures becomes the 1990s with its sonar-guided Trident missiles. The book is impervious to history and to human reading habits, which are deeply repetitive and boring. People are basically animals that know how to read.

| Speak Chinese | 茶 |
| tea | chá |

TAG PUDDING = o(o × oo)

Reading should not be about something it should be about the nohtings that occur before and after reading. As anyone who has gazed at the covers of a book over a book's lifetime can tell you, reading is a very weak pattern of information gathering and typos and it should stay that way. Or as Tom often says to his students at Oberlin College where he teaches courses in 18th-century Russian pastoral literature: "nothing ever really happens inside a book." Like an anecdote or a building w/o walls, books are the most careless and also the most relaxing of things you can do to your brain. That is why they are so beautiful and why reading and college go together so well i.e. becaues they in fact go together so poorly. Students rarely read their course assign-ments. We live in an age of rampant grade inflation. There are to many serious read-ers of literature and too few beautiful non-readers of books. What we need is more books and fewer readers. Of course, the reader of a book is like an imaginary animal in an imaginary cage, an evanescent grid whose parameters are always unchanging relative to its narrative contents. Nothing about a book should change. Each cover constitutes a stereotype of an illusion, like all those animals outside looking in who we think are us. What does it mean to look carelesly at a book? I think it means to look at one locked window and see a few identical animals inside. The beauty of a typo is that it is self-organizing.

B+/C−

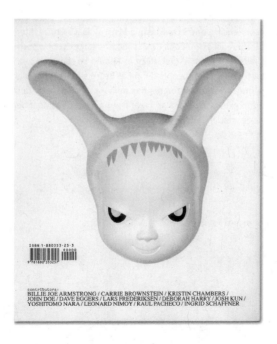

contributors:
BILLIE JOE ARMSTRONG / CARRIE BROWNSTEIN / KRISTIN CHAMBERS /
JOHN DOE / DAVE EGGERS / LARS FREDERIKSEN / DEBORAH HARRY / JOSH KUN /
YOSHITOMO NARA / LEONARD NIMOY / RAUL PACHECO / INGRID SCHAFFNER

INDEX

The realm of eros is always a bureaucracy. Bruce Pearson, a friend of mine who is a painter and a self-made gourmand, likes to buy books written by cooks whose restaurants he cannot afford to dine in. Over the past twenty-five years, he has bought dozens of books and perfectly repeated a number of dishes in them: Jean Georges Vongerichten's Sweetbreads en Cocotte with Ginger and Licorice, Thomas Keller's Bouillabaisse and Alice Waters' Grilled Duck Livers & Mustard Herb Butter Pasta. The last time I dined chez Bruce, he was wearing his painting uniform. This reminded me of Picasso and Braque who, after a long night of absinthe, would go to their studios at 8am wearing blue jumpsuits that workers in French gas stations wear. Bruce was wearing rubber sandals. When I went over last month, he served up Alain Ducasse's Provençal Leg of Lamb with Fennel and Scallion, and a Beaten Ginger Salad by Jean Georges, and I understood that it is not that recipes function as generalities, but that recipes are typologies for those feelings we have forgotten were inside us. An emotion, like a recipe, is always waiting to become the thing that it already is. The most general feelings are the most beautiful feelings because they are the only ones we know how to have. People who think they have their own emotions are incapable of empathy or cooking.

A recipe by a celebrity cook or the feelings that somebody else is having induce the most beautiful sensory hallucinations because they seem to be occurring inside of us, but they are actually only the patterns of things that somebody else has duplicated for us. The world is inconsolable. All of our emotions are obvious and the same as everybody else's. The world is consolable. Eating Bruce's version of Alice Waters' Mango Salsa was like experiencing one's own taste buds [1:1] as a form of internal emotional branding [haiku] where all extraneous details [non-haiku] exist in a permanent state of depletion. Roland Barthes said that. Recipes should be repeated just like poems. Although there were nine other people dining at Bruce's house that night, I was actually eating alone. The human tongue has millions of taste buds deposited upon it, each designed to extract a particular flavor from a food. The most beautiful book would be a 1:1 scale model of itself and divided into

Front / Back

Like a Diary of Someone I Know

WET PAINT

THANK YOU

The best way to read a book like a building is to read it over and over again. The mechanical is a system of gradual connections between dependent terms. D&G said that. Reading should be no different. Nothing is not substitutable with something else. All templates exist simultaneously, thus making the history of a book a static diagram with its own uniform past and predicted future. Roland Barthes was wrong. Like a grocery list or an anecdote, the interior of a book can be read innumerable times without damaging the contents. Things that are obvious are the most obtuse. Things that are lacking in details are the most languorous. The more generic a book is, the more consumable and lugubrious are its diagrams.

57   79   22   2   23   51   6   2   51   7   04

Like an index of meaningful moments (constraints = affects)

, [desire is about waiting for nothing]. Cookbooks are the most empty diagrams of our lives. Reading a cookbook is an exercise in extreme loneliness. [I remember when] I first moved to New York to work for Viking Penguin as a poetry slush reader in 1979. I was 22 and had just graduated from college. I first lived in Riverdale on the couch of a college friend's sister, who was an editor at *Newsweek*, and her husband, who was a college physics professor and was about to run for a Congressional seat in New Jersey. Because all of us were always at work, I hardly saw them during my stay though I think we once all went on a picnic in Central Park to hear Pavarotti. They never said a word about how my apartment search was going. Because I was young, I really did not know how long not to stay and so it took 2 months for me to excuse myself to a series of cheap hotels, first the George Washington on 23rd Street and later the Pickwick Arms Hotel on 51st Street, where I settled in for 6 months. My room did not have a kitchen but it did have a sink, for which I was grateful. This sink enabled me to keep my milk and yogurt iced for the night and to eat breakfast in the morning on my way out the door. Because there was no kitchen in my room, I usually ate dinner at Blimpies or a Greek coffee shop on the corner of 2nd Avenue and 51st Street and then came back to a hotel whose lobby and carpeted corridors were populated by bag ladies. Everything that I think about New York, the ease and difficulty and anonymity of its foods and its forms of shelter, led me to think how the city's intellectual and literary life, which I dreamed of, must also be anonymous and non-specialized, a blank form for all those things that I did not yet know. And in that way everything that I wanted for myself was already formed and routinized in that short 7-month period and would become something entirely different after that year. How many times can one change and still remain exactly who one was? I have never gone back to see whether the cheap hotel or the Greek coffee shop still stands on 51st Street and Second Avenue. What does it mean to no longer desire something like a Greek coffee shop? People fall in love with anecdotes all the time. Life is non-specialized or it ceases to exist.

For many months, when I lived at the Pickwick Arms, I went out each night at 9:30 to a newsstand on the corner of 2nd Avenue to get the next day's *Times* and when I got back to the hotel's dirty, red-carpeted lobby, I would sit there and read the apartment listings. If the paper came out on time or a little early, I would have 15 minutes to skim the ads with a red El Marko! marker and then phone people from the pay phones in the lobby, and make an appointment for first thing the next morning. And in that way, after losing a dozen or so apartments I had never seen, I finally found my first apartment: a share with an elderly German couple, the Mölls, in what was then Yorkville but which has now become just another species of white suburbia on the Upper East Side. I lived and slept for months in their beige bedroom while they lived in their white-carpeted living room. I paid $225 a month, which was less than the $700 a month I paid at the Pickwick Arms. Mr. Möll was a retired baker for Kleine Konditorei and Mrs. Möll was a housewife who I think must have worked as a beautician since one of the first things she offered me was to cut my hair on Sunday mornings. I thought at the time this was very kind and I still do but I now think she thought my hair was too long and didn't suit the look of the apartment. A 50s kitchen with a beautiful German oven, I think it was a Küppersbusch, separated their section of the apartment from mine and also gave me a simultaneous route to the front door and the bathroom, both of which we shared. My own family—my mother, my father and my sister, who were living in Athens, Ohio, and in New Haven, Connecticut—never came to visit me at this apartment. What is that something in a story that keeps waiting to direct the story beyond itself,

5

to a kind of annulment or anomaly? Like most people who live in other people's houses, I was only allowed to do certain things at certain hours. Most importantly or perhaps least importantly in retrospect, I was only allowed to cook meals for myself before 8:30 pm, and since I was always out at the Old Town or some other bar after work, I rarely made it home in time to cook for myself. I would usually buy a sandwich from a deli nearby or at a store which sold a kind of hoagie called a Blimpie. They were delicious and so large that I could usually get two meals out of a single Blimpie. When I came home late at night I had a small desk where I would eat a leftover Blimpie and write a poem on a blue IBM Selectric that I had used in college. And so I made myself unthinkingly a schedule of drinking, eating out, looking for apartments, and occasionally getting my hair cut and writing a poem if the time saw fit. It is odd but I do not think I ever had a Chinese take-out that first year in New York even though I now think the Chinese food in New York is among the best I have ever eaten, with the possible exception of the restaurants in Taipei. Because I had very little money that year, I bought only two books between September, when I started work-ing at Viking Penguin, and December of 1981. What is that something in a story that keeps waiting to

On rare occasions when I did cook, it was usually under the tutelage of Mr. Möll, his wife, and the first cookbook I ever owned, which is probably the only book I really think about when I think about myself growing into an adult. I did not after all want to be a beggar at my table. The book is *James Beard's Theory and Practice of Good Cooking*. The only other book I kept in that apartment at the time was a copy of *Self-Portrait in a Convex Mirror* by John Ashbery, which I had stolen from Viking Penguin when I had interned there the summer before. Some of these dates may not be quite right. The Beard book was a beautiful book. First of all it was a hardcover and had a dust jacket. Secondly, I had stolen it from a fancy bookstore on Madison Avenue. It was the first hardcover cookbook I ever owned and the first cookbook I ever stole, so it was the beginning of a corrupt library de haute cuisine. I read it nearly every night while at the Mölls'. I am not sure why I was so engrossed in it since I cooked so rarely, but I think it had to do with becoming what I perceived was a classy New Yorker. I don't know exactly what I was waiting for while I was growing up and reading and re-reading that book and not cooking much, but I know I was waiting for something, and whenever I look at a painting (I am a very good cook) or write a poem (I am a pretty good poet), it is hard for me not to remember the *Theory and Practice of Good Cooking* and what James Beard said about how you should touch a steak with your hand in order to tell if it is done and that the color of food was the best way to taste it in advance. When I write a poem I often think of the hand that touches a steak to tell if it's done.

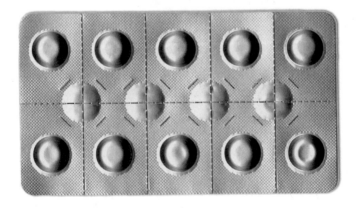

It is best to write about nothing or something that is dead when one is writing. It is only in that way that one can write about oneself. For the seven months I camped out with the Mölls—before I finally decided to give up on the publishing business and go back to grad school at Columbia—I worked my way gradually through a quarter of the recipes, learning how to burn butter, cook a steak on a stove top (I knew how to barbeque in Ohio), and ultimately how to eat by myself without too many other feelings intruding on the life I was living at the moment. The most beautiful deregulated things in a cookbook are the things that are left out, and of course those things are our feelings, which exist to be deregulated. Of course, only a feeling that has been regulated knows what it means to be deregulated.

Alice B. Toklas's cookbook, *The Alice B. Toklas Cookbook*, published in 1954 by Harper & Brothers, was her first. My copy has an orange cloth binding and a green spine stamped with gold and orange letters up and down the spine. My copy is missing a good chunk of its white dust wrapper, which is alternately green, orange, brown and mustard. But the most beautiful thing about the book are its omissions. In the first American edition, there is a lovely tipped-in erratum slip alerting the reader of the faux pas of peas, which are entirely left out from the recipe for Peas à la Française. Besides that little slip of paper, my favorite chapters are "Food in the United States in 1934 and 1935" because I was not around to know the feelings of food that year, and "Food in French Homes" because food in French homes is always better than food out of those same homes. If you compare the American edition with the British first edition published by Michael Joseph in 1945, you will note that the American edition lacks a crucial recipe: Hashish Fudge.

Later that year or early in the next year, I bought my first Chinese cookbook, a cheap British Penguin that I got for 48 cents on one of the metal outdoor carts at the Strand. This book had a picture of a huge pig carcass hanging from somewhere, which I did not like because I thought it gave Chinese people and Chinese food the appearance of modern-day primitives who keep pigs in their backyards and hang them from porches (I think differently now about that cover) and while I read this book in tandem with the Beard book, I never cooked from it because the recipes did not seem at all Chinese. The language of "Cooking in Chinese in China" and "Cooking in Chinese Abroad" were bipolar chapters that seemed to come abruptly, one from another century and one from another continent. Like most cookbooks, this two-in-one book was about repression and memory disorders. The language was arch, old-fashioned, colonial and depressing because the English used to describe pressed ducks and soy sauce and stir-fry and soup in dumpling or tin wok seemed too nostalgic to actually eat a meal in. What is the use of a language if you cannot consume it? The language of true Chinese cooking is very spare and very very thin, just like a recipe or a very fine novel. To be able to eat in Chinese you must also be able to cook in Chinese. To be able to cook in Chinese you must be able to see the food first. There was no mention of what a scallion pancake looked like when it was fried or what bean paste should taste like when it was fresh [uncooked]. There is always so much irreconcilable information in a cookbook. As anyone who cooks can tell you, the longer a recipe, the more miniscule the finished dish will be. Yet I found in the book the most apt metaphor for Chinese food. In the first chapter on ingredients, the author remarks: cornstarch is the glue that holds all Chinese food together. When I told this to my mother she just laughed and laughed and said:

That is very true

OR:

That is a load of nonsense (hoo sha ba dao)
緊\1髭胖

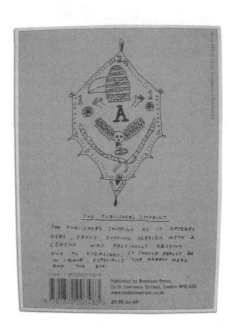

THE PUBLISHERS IMPRINT

THE PUBLISHERS IMPRINT AS IT APPEARS
HERE, PROUD, EVOKING HERALDIC MYTH &
LEGEND WAS PREVIOUSLY ABSENT
DUE TO OVERSIGHT. IT SHOULD REALLY BE
IN COLOUR, ESPECIALLY THE PARROT HEAD
AND THE EYE.

ISBN 1-870003-48-9

Published by Redstone Press,
7a St Lawrence Terrace, London W10 5SU
www.redstonepress.co.uk

£4.99 inc VAT

SKU

The best books are the ones that read like paintings, and the best paintings are the ones that read like quotation marks. As Pater (and Plato before him) noted, painting and poetry are forms of cultural impatience and the uninhabitable. As such they function like historical diagrams in verso or photographic negatives. They punctuate given space with hallucinogenic color because they are in color. For example, painting is dead or painting is beautiful because it generates one word after another.

Verlag der Buchhandlung Walther König, Köln

UNIFORM

Prada
Functional fragrances

Books without authors
Empathy

Precise times of readings
Myth control

doppelgangers
NORAD

Tool-books
Intensity-books

sophia
How to Cook and Eat in Chinese

"zero mass of events"
"errors vs. death"

Genre Rules:
Cosmetic Nomenclature

Hapax 2
Prison Campuses

Topothesia
Haldol

Moveable filters
formal/informal

Atmospheric Foliage
Working Class Sports Knowledge

Thins W/O
Architecture of Addiction

"Outlines"
Weightlessness

Recursive Systems
Card

Why Do Englishmen
InfraSound

[program exit]   1970
QNS   *Bible* from memory

insert   dummy
Pandemonium   educational filmstrip

J   things to buy w / my Crestar VISA
if-added methods   cultural capital

HighLighter   somebody to see poetry
Locke   Memory Occlusion

Moribund Pedagogy   More Perfection
Sheath cables   v.

DIY   Ref. Amateurism
reified idea: Semiotic Agents

Gospel   acid test
Puppy   "my own glosses"

8 sets per page   "exacting"
memoir vs. diary   under what basis

A Dictionary of Systems Theory

AMERICAN STANDARD CODE for INFORMATION EXCHANGE

Being on reality TV is the newest format of class-based identity branding in which people become goods, work is alchemically "removed" from life, and labor is camouflaged as a mediated, i.e., prime-time, leisure format. On a show like *The Apprentice*, everyday contestants give up real, often lucrative jobs as stockbrokers, exotic dancers, real-estate salespersons or cigar-store owners to compete for a $250,000 one-year job with Donald Trump. Of course, they're not really giving up work, they're giving up leisure. Unlike sit-coms where actors *pretend* to live everyday lives, individuals on *The Apprentice* are a new class of non-unionized, marginally paid "non-actors" who pretend not to work even as they are *always* working the life that generates ratings or publicity—sleeping [in Trump Plaza], playing golf [at Trump National Golf Course], etc. In the world of reality TV, non-perfomative, i.e., non-distributed, forms of labor do not exist.

Like most perishable products, reality TV "jobs" are assets with fixed expiration dates (someone is fired every week). What the contestants "buy" or gamble with their on-screen labor is a measured dose of exposure. Unlike real celebrities who have life spans that can measure in decades, reality TV contestants are programmed in advance by the networks to have a much shorter (a single season) and more unpleasant bout with celebrity illness. Reality TV stars, in effect, rent fame. Being on reality TV thus evinces the pathology of what options traders term a wasting asset. Boardroom sessions are allowed to drag on for hours, inducing fatigue and "unpredictable" outbursts; contestants' beds are cut shorter than average to make sleep more difficult, and contestants are goaded during filming. But just in case the networks are wrong and a contestant goes on to more lasting fame, the networks require contestants to sign contracts entitling producers to a percentage of profits. Hence a new class of wage slave is born. Soap opera actors own their own futures and are guaranteed a SAG wage—but reality TV non-stars work for next to nothing and sell out their future earnings potential in advance. When is a celebrity not a true celebrity? When she's on reality TV. To counter this, the networks create the illusion that a contestant's "job" endures posthumously beyond the show's time slot—after being fired, contestants appear the next day with Katie Couric on the *Today* show.

Of course, only people who can afford the luxury of not working (for pay) for the six weeks of filming could even make it to New York, and the program's middle- and upper-middle-class bias is consistent with late 19th-century sociological practices, where the burgeoning affluent class's lack of connection to manual labor led to curious feelings of life as unreal and to the first series of "objective" undercover investigations of the working class by upper-class participant observers. Kwame and Heidi and Omarosa—or rather, the reality TV genre—constitute the Jacob Riises of our era, with one key difference. Rather than contemplate the working class, the contestants on *The Apprentice* examine themselves, or more particularly, their fantasies about their working lives and the administered workspace—which is transformed into a TV game show. Or to put it in terms that both working viewer and working contestant can relate to: the ultimate fantasy island is the self-mediated workspace with only one survivor—a boss introjected [as oneself].

When asked why they work for nothing (they receive room and board) and live under the threat of a weekly pink slip, contestants almost unanimously reply that they are doing it in exchange for "the experience." That experience, even if it is a post-mortem (broadcast) event, is considered priceless. The future may not be realizable, but its promise endures long after it has died. Of course, it is hard to assign a precise dollar value to an experience, especially its life and eventual death on TV before 21 or 27 million viewers. Like most commodities that promise to deliver something they cannot (drinking Pepsi won't really make you a part of the new Pepsi generation), being a celebrity [like having a dream job, losing 250 pounds, or going out with a supermodel] for your average American is an oxymoron or else it is very short-lived. Hence just beyond the range of quantification. Hence the unquenchable desire to do the math. If the dollar value of the televised experience is a cipher (or at least incalculable on a standard adding machine), then its short-lived nature is transformative: it is the perfect surface for a working out in the form of a fantasy. This the game-show format happily provides as a cutthroat weekly do-or-die cycle of catharsis and psychoanalysis whose primary aim is mathematical: subtract one contestant weekly; reward the others with a stay-of-execution meal or a round of golf. Whew I made it through another week!

The promised life span or duration of any commodity is a source of considerable financial and philosophical speculation. Such speculations do not materialize on air. Kwame does not ask: "When will I be fired (from a job I don't even have yet)? Will I be unemployable in the financial sector after my stint on reality TV?" Like the fantasmatic "real thing" that a sip of Coke promises and that advertisers cultivate in the consumer, the experience promised by commodities is a void that the commodity manages to only partly conceal. As occupational life therapy, shopping or reality TV will only take one so far. Our future experiences—commodified and made "real" by being broadcast—are experiential voids, non-happenings, mathematically impossible formulas that are arrayed around our identities, which also look disturbingly like voids. For all its declarations of reality, reality TV broadcasts the future as an unknowable fairy-tale ending—but an ending nonetheless. Deep down inside, we all know reality TV is unreal. The most real experience is being fired or turning off the TV. The show thus has the paradoxical effect of making everyone want to tune in and work overtime and generate higher ratings. Viewers resemble contestants who frantically sell lemonade, rent out apartments, conduct golf tournaments, organize benefit pop concerts, run a pedicab business, or travel around Manhattan looking for the lowest spot price on an ounce of gold. Nobody wants to be fired from his or her life.

What is the promise of work? In America, work offers the fantasy of filling the void, i.e., erasing the routinization of a 9-to-5 job. Thus being a celebrity becomes the newest "job" in America. Warhol noted that being beautiful takes work. Reality TV exploits

(continued on page 222)

The history of architecture, dining out, cosmetics, and reading boils down to a small number of "effects": incandescent lightbulbs, forced-air heating, load-bearing walls, the restaurant and its menu, synthetic scents like Chanel No. 5, nouvelle cuisine, declassified information, three-martini lunches, conspicuous consumption, fluorescent lighting, thermostats and climate-control systems, the escalator, moveable type, hypertext, fluorescent lighting, the quarto, the Usenet, *Le guide Michelin* (1900), fast food, the internet, task lighting, Zagat guides, junk food, pulse-code modulation, fusion food, central air (1902), newsbyte, and conceptual dining.

The history of reality TV boils down to the recirculation of a limited number of "TV effects." Most reality TV formats are camouflaged, mildly interactive artifacts — conveying way-of-life information in the manner of natural history museum dioramas with laugh tracks. Reality TV programs appear genre-less, i.e., they blend various genres — sit-com, soap opera, game show, serious drama, confession, talk show, dating show, documentary, and live sporting event. In this way they disguise the pervasiveness of television and of mediated life in general and suggest the fluidity of all genres as they expand into what is known as "an experience": that drifting atemporality and spatial unfixedness that is everyday life. In this way, nostalgia is preconditioned and occurs around things that have not actually transpired. The laugh track is replaced by the instantaneous monitoring of an audience. And this in turn suggests, like a kind of mask, that all experiences, especially the most personal, have already happened, conversationally speaking, or do not become "real" until broadcast. Thus the *American Idol* from spring 2004 merges a hyper-bland talent show with soap opera, talk show, and sporting event featuring instant replays, post-performance rundowns, mock coaching sessions, Internet discussion groups, and Olympic-style direct voting that most viewers associate with live sports broadcasts. The underlying assumption of media monitoring is that the viewers, not the networks, are responsible for manufacturing the next American idol, and thus simultaneously producing exactly what they consume. As recent experiments with "breathable food" [dust-blown muesli, aerosol-based vegetables, "Pharma Food" (Guixé), and vitamin/mineral patches] indicate, food, like pop stars, can be transmitted and consumed as information.

The processes of information "aggregation, filtering, and transmission" [Fukuyama, Shulsky] become simultaneous "conditions." Thus *Idol* is live and includes a [non-televised] voting session, and a follow-up broadcast that repeats portions of the previous night's show and tallies the voting results. Mediation is no longer grounded in differing formats or objects (converting painting into sculpture or book into film) but in a single, cross-mediated event. Reality mediates reality. TV mediates non-TV reality. Everything we see is instantaneously repeated as real life. That is why it is virtually impossible to watch a reality TV series over again — that would add an unnecessary layer of mediation. Of course, as any person under 30 can tell you, reality is a highly mediated generational category. The networks have provided a "real" format where 20-something and 30-something consumers choose idols in the manner that Henry Ford engineered the Model T so that consumers would have no choice, where all individual consumer choices are cosmetic alterations on the surface of the same generic product. In that way, all choices like all moods are possible, and none exist outside the boundaries of the show itself. Unlike the 19th century where the proliferation of the novel, the penny dreadfuls and serial novels in newspapers were the norms for emotional information processing, in our era of proliferating information, fact is cheaper and faster to distribute than fiction. People make real choices in order to experience highly mediated [diffused] emotions.

The first run of reality TV programming suggests the next marketing trend: selling consumers not goods but increasingly intangible forms of diffused or altered/recycled information identity back to them. Hence, programs about "being" a celebrity (Paris Hilton's *The Simple Life, The Osbornes*); being a boxer (*The Contender*); being someone else (*Extreme Makeover, The Swan*); being rich and/or being in love (*Joe Millionaire, My Big Fat Obnoxious Fiancé, For Love or Money, Blind Date, The Bachelor, The Fifth Wheel*); being a thrill seeker (*Fear Factor, Survivor, Jackass*); being a live-action hero (*Next Action Star* and its "real" TV movie spin-off, *Bet Your Life*) or even the most intangible form of identity known as [being oneself and having an] everyday [i.e., no] life (*The Real World, Road Rules, Big Brother*). Even *Gilligan's Island* is being made into a "reality format," where the once-fictional generic characters become real-life generic characters: professor, aspiring actress, farm girl, skipper/construction worker, klutz-nerd, millionaire + wife. The premise is that only by inserting everyday people into canned television formats and genres can the viewer's experience of TV be made "real" again. No longer do viewers watch fictional characters or famous actors, as in *Leave It to Beaver* or *Ozzie and Harriet,* where the characters remind them of themselves. They watch real people who, by *not* acting, remind the viewers of themselves acting like themselves.

In such a world of identity branding and diffusion, everyone becomes the human equivalent of an entertainment bar code, data celebrity or Human Muzak (Humak): data "working" 24 hours a day to be transmitted to someone else in exchange for something "real." In the information age, wage slavery is superceded by information servants, "rental" or "generic" celebrities (an off-brand of true celebrities, who, in point of fact, are *both* rich and famous and don't need to race around town to buy gold bars or Big Berthas for a deferred prize). Post-consumer demographic data will thus replace old-fashioned and impoverished forms of anonymous personal identity. A new class of individuals arises: Anonymous Celebrities who "act" as if their labor has a zero valuation and who offer their labor in exchange for a dose of exposure. As the Amex slogan nostalgically goes: "Membership has its rewards."

BAR CODE Buildings

Unlike a building, a bar code is impossible to hallucinate. Mies was right. The edges of human laboriousness can be made to evaporate into things that do not exist. A building should have a highly controlled vocabulary. Its temporal dimension should be uniform from the inside out. In that way, buildings can be outlines of buildings, just as, at any given time, the Broadway musical *Cats* casts its own shadow, a rehearsal stopping and starting up in multiple time zones across the globe (circa 1997) like the rerun of a live event.

Unlike department stores and shopping malls, and before them the arcades, open-air markets and public theatres, today's superstores are autonomous and deregulated every minute of the day just like the colors that decorate the surfaces of commodities. In that way they appear to be constantly changing and constantly standing still like abandoned shipping yards or unused tennis courts. Being inside a store like Wal-Mart, Bed Bath & Beyond, Home Depot or Sam's Club, where you can find nearly everything under one roof, is like being in a wandering bar code, a 21st-century variant of the cargo cult, where global inventory levels are tracked at checkout and transmitted directly to manufacturers, thus eliminating inventory stockpiling and other market inefficiencies. Anything that cannot be counted and measured ceases to exist. Consumers enter the supply chain as inventory requests or data events, which are no longer subject to utilization as software commands or as passive data to be mined by corporations, but *issue* commands and dictate production. Information, like propaganda, ceases to be passive. Producers and retail outlets are merely the logic gates through which data events and hardware choices are routed and "produced" [ex post facto]. Since irresolvable desires are the most inefficient of market forces in centralized systems, they become irrelevant. The store drifts. Data defiles description. A chain store, like a book, will slow down a human desire almost to the point of stopping, in the same way that goats or sheep, after given LSD, will promenade in predictable geometric forms: triangles, rectangles, ovals, half-squares, circles, X-forms, figure-Ls and figure 8s. Hence the tendency to package exactly the same product, as with Apple iPods, in a psychedelic rainbow hue of colors. Variation is the mantra of the new standardization.

LOOSELY TYPED LANGUAGE

Supply-chain monitoring and spikes in consumption *within* a single superstore
are the closest things to watching a [standardized] sunset or thunderstorm erupt
within minutes of each other in a space that somehow contains them both. Time as
seasonal roundelay or linear progression is disaggregated by simultaneous flashes on
different sectors of a selling floor. Like starlight seen from above, consumption events
are mutating codes rather than hierarchical control structures. A generic template is
a template that is migrating somewhere else. Like a Botox-injected forehead, which
is temporarily paralyzed by a bacterium (*C. botulinum*) and surrenders its lexicon of
signified facial meanings to which it was once connected, every section of a Wal-Mart
Supercenter comprises an entry-less index or aerial mosaic in a glass box—where
all sections are lit uniformly and where all differences are absorbed by repetition.
Grocery, Electronics, Family Hair Salon, One-Hour Photo, Tire & Lube Express, Family
Vision Center, Lawn & Garden, Pharmacy Department, Health & Beauty, Baby World,
Sporting Goods, Auto, Kitchen and Bath—flourish as diagrams for the redundant
lifestyle phases of the consumer. Consumers no longer have identities; they wait
for them to repeat ad nauseum. Ceilings and floors [subroutines] disappear into
girders whose off-white colors are indistinguishable from the stores' cream-colored
awnings, taupe-colored shelves, and pumice-shaded floor tiles. Everyone in Wal-Mart
wears pants. Everyone's pants are beige [   ]. In a post-monarchist system like
Wal-Mart, everything is electronically tagged [variant record] infrastructure, except the
architecture. In the future, all Wal-Marts will be on wheels and will be driven to "new"
rural areas as the need arises. Such premonitory spaces [like the lifestyle zones on a
Wal-Mart selling floor] are "places" where the future has "already happened." Such
spaces are beautiful because very little memory can be retrieved from them. Each
zone of the selling floor rises into nothing and behaves like a cage for desire, in the
same way that the more ornamental aspects of family life

[Family Vacation, Infancy, Little League, Childhood, Preparatory School, PTA, Girl
Scouts, School Picnic, Home Ec, Shop]

PHP CODE

```
<META name="description" content="This is description field">
<meta name="keywords" content="about, friends, family">
```

once did. [As the ads go, Wal-Mart is one big family]

As the largest private-sector employer on the planet, Wal-Mart's roughly 3,800 stores and 591 Sam's Clubs, are a reconstituted Second Nature [Family Structure] or ecological theatre run backwards. In this brand of eco-tourism, inhabitants who worked in local stores put out of business by Wal-Mart are re-hired by a Wal-Mart, where they are consolidated, scheduled to work no more than 34 hours a week, and paid the minimum wage. Visiting Wal-Mart is like taking a climate-controlled walking tour of a displaced, third-world community within a global economy. Unlike most third-world economies where scale is down-sized and community spaces are fractioned and crammed with humans, a Wal-Mart *openly* camouflages this fracture by disguising employees as good neighbors and by consolidating goods in aisles as wide and as flat as (former) Main Streets or prairies, all of which rest under a warehouse vault with skylights. A Wal-Mart inverts the secretive black-box mentality that underlies stealth buildings, whose interiors and data cables are sheathed in triple-thick copper and whose exterior is a mirrored glass box—draped around a concrete bunker.

#pilsner is my favourite kind of #beer

As with their precursor the shopping mall, superstores are based on totalization and its mimicry: exclusion, flatness, invisible centralization, instantaneous access to goods, zero discordance, visible infrastructures, long sight-lines [vista], no surplus, disappearing exits, "aggressive hospitality" and dispersal. Just as the praying mantis becomes a stick that its prey sees "through," so too with the wall-less layout of most superstores. (There are no walls in Wal-Mart.) Nobody tries to steal anything. *Trying* to find a salesperson in Wal-Mart is like finding a police officer in a ghost town or a clown in a department store. In this sense, the poorer citizens (Invisible, i.e., Dressed up in Uniforms), the infrastructure of the downtown city (Contracting or Out of Business) and beyond that the global market (Inventory Expansion) have all migrated *inside* the building/working warehouse, which is only nominally a building but an approximation [optical illusion] of one.

Power loves a vacuum because it is theatrical and creates voids [of itself] ad nau-
seum. Power loves a labyrinth because it is theatrical and creates voids [of something
else] in limited quantities. Social norms are enforced with the "10-foot rule" (talk to
anyone who comes within a 10-foot radius) AND the "Sundown Rule" (sell everything
the customer needs before sundown) OR (delay the store's closing time). For this
reason, Bar Code Buildings are also known as Flawed Power Approximations or
data points. An Approximate Building flashes into existence whenever a consumer
"chooses" a product superstitiously, like a symptom. All choices are freely uninten-
tional and freely made. Mass individualization is the new standard. Muteness rules.
What you hear is what you hear. In that way, everything is unrecognizable even though
out in the open. Thus, a "phenomenological reduction" marked by "reduced listening"
[Husserl], thoughtlessness, and under-contextualization. As in the rain forest so too
with the shopping mall: no sound is produced [to be heard]

(shopping carts, re-stocking of shelves, bar-code scanners, babies crying)

Every era manufactures the most beautiful and concealed forms of political inertia,
impersonality, and apathy (ours are shopping and reading and architecture), and in
this way creates the obvious routes to the freedom it imagines. Only the freedom born
of boredom [not having any real ideas] is worth having. Only the freedom born of
boredom [not having any real desires] is worth having. The most beautiful desires are
intentionless, fleeting and empty, like mass entertainment. Picasso loved the circus
and the harlequin. Duchamp loved the hardware store and the Erlenmeyer flask. Most
of Duchamp's works are meant to collect dust or disappear behind a flat veil
of optical simulations. Rhetorics of total freedom are a product of cold-war liberalism
and need to be jettisoned in favor of rhetorics of precise measurement and control,
which as Adorno noted, "absorb the mind completely." Today our desires are the
latent mythology (a standard stoppage) underlying the generic format known as
a book, a painting or a Wal-Mart superstore. Most of our neuroses are blank. We
would do well not to choose our symptoms very wisely.

Bewes, 105

II

Most Bar Code Buildings recirculate on the surface of suburban and rural landscapes, but there has been a migration toward cities, where structures evaporate directly *into* being *out* of information or, in the cases of companies like Enron and Adelphia and PSINet, out of disinformation, accounting undulations, mergers, and chapter 11 filings. Unlike the first round of shopping-mall development, which was fueled by "accelerated depreciation" tax codes in 1954, the new stadium buildings reflect changes in economic sponsorship. In major cities like Houston, Dallas and San Francisco, the expansion of Bar Code Buildings takes the form of naming rights assigned to already existing buildings, usually the largest buildings on the urban landscape such as stadiums or convention centers. Thus the Texas Rangers play at Ameriquest Field, in exchange for having their yearly mortgage paid by the lending company giant. Likewise the Washington Redskins play at FedExField, the Atlanta Hawks and Thrashers play the Philips Arena, and the Dallas Mavericks and Stars work out of the American Airlines Arena. Just as bar codes can be applied to everything: honeybees, rental cars, checked luggage, heat tiles on NASA shuttles, nuclear waste in transit, tattoos (Japan) and even fashion models during runway shows, Bar Code Buildings are an identification code, as well as a pictorial representation or symbol for that code. Increasingly, a building's physical symbol structure remains visibly unchanged while its underlying information [ID] code changes. Thus when Enron went bust, the Houston Astros no longer played at Enron Field but Minute Maid Park. Most Bar Code Buildings, like stadiums, have an average expiration date of 30 years. In this way, a building's structural loop persists long after the building's codes become illegible, disappear altogether, or fade into something more generic, as with the Adelphia Coliseum, now known by Nashvillians simply as the Coliseum. Like the idea of truth and the feelings we confuse with it, Ebbets Field, Yankee Stadium, Tiger Stadium, and Fenway Park are outmoded pictorial concepts. In this they resemble the book, which is the exemplary product of an age when information was proprietary, hygienic, and stable. A book should be the weakest information pattern that is visible to the eye. Only in that way can it outlive its data.

CLOSET

1404

OPEN AREA

1406

[Today] a work of architecture [or film] or [poem] or [painting] or [novel] should have as fluid and standardized an ID [OBJECT ID™ SYSTEM] as possible and function like a waiting area, time slot, universal market/currency or metadata standard. The best waiting areas today are located in books and airports, where traveling = waiting time = non-activity. Being in an airport is the closest we can come to being stranded on a grid. Now I am flying to Tokyo. Now I am flying to [   ] Reykjavik. The conflation of space with surface, and interior with exterior areas mirrors the condition of cognitive capitalism, where nothing appears to be occurring outside the system boundaries [glass curtain walls] and where it is difficult to make distinctions between pre- and post-consumptive objects or their desires. The speed of commodification should be uniform. Conditions replace spatial elements. As anyone who has been to an airport can tell you: all forms of excitement are moribund forms of pre-excitement. Details become generalities. Everything obtuse is obvious.

Airports are the slowest of typologies or indeterminate structures of waiting. They are conducive to suspended-time activities like shopping, reading, being bored, watching TV, getting drunk, or eating "fast" food. Waiting in an airport is an inverse form of reg- ulation just as breathing and letter writing once were. From a contextual standpoint, most airports are almost exactly the same and only the presence of a colored logo here (Shiseido, Virgin Atlantic) or directional sign there (Cairo, Nairobi, Dallas/Fort Worth) tells you where you were or which flight you had forgotten to board. Missing a flight is the newest species of memory recovery. Change is indistinguishable from stasis. Hence passengers tend to buy wasting assets in an airport: luxury items and other counter-stimulants to amnesia—perfume, alcohol or cigarettes—products that realize their potential after their cellophane or wax seals are broken and they burn off or evaporate away.

In this way, all emotions like commodities can evaporate more rapidly outwards into parameters for other emotions or genres of emotions. Buildings resemble receipts or home furnishings. Shopping malls modulate into airports and street-level museum stores. Books like food become atmospheric. Restaurants resemble agro-stops or farms. Breads and pastry buns, tarts, cakes, etc. look like jewelry or architecture. The campus morphs into a warehouse learning outlet. Lemon meringue becomes rock opera. Writing a novel is a variant of writing a poem. Sculptures devolve into shampoo containers, ingredient lists, menus, domestic appliances, or, at the other extreme, dust [*Large Glass* 1915–23], soap bubbles, children and their toys, temporary folders or document history lists, food art like Robert Gober's doughnuts, or numerous blow-away, post-combustible (ash) art forms. A cigarette is a controlled fire whose fuel is dosed to emit nicotine at a standard rate. As Dieter Rot said of his chocolate sculptures: "The worms and bugs in my pieces are my employees. You must not disturb them; they have to do their job like any one of us." The most beautiful works deplete or eat information at regulated intervals just as a magnetic tape will gradually surrender all but the outlines of its audible information. Time of this reading: "exactly" 34 minutes. As any non-collector of dust or cookbooks can tell you, if the amount of packaged [consumable] information is decreased, entropy will increase.

I was dining at Per Se, Thomas Keller's immaculate restaurant spin-off in New York, where I was served a minimalist bouillon by no fewer than 7 waiters. The room was fussy and minimal. The bouillon was made out of veal bones that had been carved by kitchen artisans into 40 precise 1-inch cubes, and then boiled for exactly 4 hours, thus allowing for maximum gelatin extraction with minimum boil off. In Keller's kitchen nothing is left to chance. Everything is subject to precise rules of repetition, which act as a flavor enhancer. Childhood, having long vanished, returns for seconds. Everything one eats is exactly the same as the last time one was there. For this reason, it is necessary to eat in Keller's restaurants repeatedly to reinforce the overwhelming sense of etiquette, normality and banality of one's feelings. Deleuze was wrong. Emotions can be geometrically crafted to repeat perfectly. The repetition of a work of art like an emotion is like a generality [recipe] without a concept [   ]

FOWL

Fowls are variable [   ] commercial structures such as newsstands, parking garages, self-storage units, gas stations, bus shelters, quick flat-fix shops, drive-thru wedding chapels, and car washes. These minimally staffed or self-service structures are generally all-door all-floor, open 24 hours a day, and give off a continuous generic message. With their diluted, envelope-like structures and environmentally evasive designs, Fowls are not subject to historic preservation laws, are immune from becoming "historical" and are continually on the verge of vanishing or being razed so that more profitable buildings can be put up in their place. As most of our desires are weak today, Fowls tend to be under-noticed. Yet Fowls are among the most atmospheric building species because they function as taxonomic labels or brands for spaces we might have inhabited.

POEM

HOUSE # 7

(SCALE: $^1/_4$" TO 1')

Dear_____,

What is an unlivable house?

I wanted to make a house out of white out + little bit

of the ocean stalled between

walls as type from bathtub to bathtab

S + A +   N + D

Some hinge the slipper

The following is a statistical summary that can be used to generate names:

20 fives 1 one   12 threes   7 sixes

It begins to snow from my front porch

POSTSCRIPT :

I can see my mother from the front porch.

MOSS

What are the less than decisive frontiers and decorative surface tectonics of American reading today? Newsstands, coffee kiosks, food courts, shoe-shine stands, duty-free shops, public restrooms, etc. appear to us as intimate hallucinations, folding fonts, tropes [holes], scripted interfaces [pockets], or protocol sentences [shade] distributed evenly across the surface of airports, train stations, ground floors of hospital wait-ing areas, and other public spaces, especially corridors, where it grazes, unlooked at and lacking "incident." Nomadic, Moss disperses indoors, perfumed through the floors of large corporate offices like a schedule arranging and re-arranging its décor against a backdrop of open cubicles, conference rooms, pods, supply closets, unisex washrooms, employee lounges, office suites, or stalls that beget further variability and surface treatments. What is an office but a series of facsimiles, internal memos, candlestick charts, calendars, bar graphs, zip-code maps, Post-its, and questionnaires circulated in a place where all communication and announcements are filtered as inter alia background. Moss encompasses any Mobile Optical Semiotic Surface where privacy is attenuated and *hypotyposis* results.

Like architectural experiences and most of our non-emotions, i.e., emotions we haven't had yet or emotions we've already had, Moss substitutes for a sense of place, which is just detail that interrupts a non-homogeneous experience. Expenditure [all expenditures are equal] and going out a gate to catch a plane are mirrored activities in atopia. Recent public art, particularly at airports, reminds us of an algebraic version of Moss, or what Baudelaire, speaking of drunkenness and anticipating the Breathalyzer, labeled a number. A Donald Judd serial sculpture is a perfect [pre-fabricated] retinal outline (ghost of painting) for the replicating, absent, machine-stamped auto body parts and artificial colors of a commercial painting system that was once correlated to particular models of automobiles and Harleys. Thus the mysterious intoxication of a Judd sculpture devolves from a mathematical problem: something is repeated and transmitted to us, like an idea vacillating on our retina and waiting for its signifier to materialize. In an airport, who remembers the things one buys or wanted to buy on the way to somewhere else [sense flow]? Who remembers the color of the airplanes [diagram flow] one has flown on?

OFF / ON

Like form itself, color "begins" where it no longer corresponds to natural coloration or organic form. Eisenstein said that. As Judd realized, metallic motorcycle paints can be applied very thinly to aluminum sheets. In that way, color, like a logo [corporate Moss], functions as a layer of information applied to the visual anthropology of everyday life. Color is a boundary in a world that is fully administered [incandescent]. Because it erases the labor of the craftsman who made it and renders its material form into something projected and insubstantial, a Judd sculpture is an open format [code] for a vanished painting or dematerialized sculpture. Like skateboard connoisseurs who regard all abandoned and disused sites as feedback loops, in terms of their skateability and transformation into thrash pipes or funboxes, Judd understood that information should never be allowed to accumulate for too long [like desires] and become a static form. Information should constitute the thinnest possible coating on paintings, sculptures, deserted public plazas, and airports. In such a way, forms that disappear become extensions of everything else. What you see is what you do not see. Thus, between a Judd sculpture and a series of abandoned artillery sheds in Marfa is an inaudible line.

What is the difference between something hallucinated and something actually seen? An idea of decentralization. Desiring is a form of hallucinating information. Desiring less is a way of hallucinating more. A Judd sculpture is an after-image that happens to be an object surrounded by a space or a Judd object is an extremely transient event that "invokes" protocols and linked procedures which [functional simplification] pare down information in the manner of a Gaussian curve. Everything that is beautiful is generic. Everything that is beautiful is generic. A beautiful book would be a self-organizing collection (*florilegia*, schedule, photo album, digest of meals, itinerary) of non-events. Like most mathematicians, Judd was an optimist by default.

MORE / LESS

In the mind of Judd or a child schooled in the geometric grids of the German *kindergarten*, the world of color is an awakening and a recognition that looking has its own frequencies: a chair in its place has abstract, mystical properties that allow it to assume the identity of a finite number, a crystal or even a door. Every one of Judd's "objects" functions in at least 3 or 4 different ways: as furniture, as painting, as sculpture, sound-mirror, as phase-based music, as landscape, information template, etc. That is the beauty of a rectilinear surface [valence] and its planar substitutions. Most cylinders and ovals will disappear from Judd's work by 1966 because, as forms, they are insufficiently two-dimensional, suggest too much movement and are not "oblique" or "shallow" enough [as descriptions or templates] "like" a painting. How does one turn something off that is already off? How does one make something more into something less? Everything that is beautiful is generic. For those who live on the surface of information, anyone can be a dog on the internet. "My thought comes from painting even if I don't paint."

No data is free. As Turing recognized, the ideal computer is imaginary. The ideal Judd sculpture functions like a thermostat. It imparts the illusion of solving a problem. After 1963, Judd paints no more paintings. The *idea* of Less Information [in the field of painting] = more uncertainty = reduced feedback = > manifestations of patterned chaos in another system: that 3-dimensional space between a painting system and a sculpture system. Nothing white can be truly minimal or flat. No one has yet undertaken a study of the low-frequency, musical resonances emitted by the colors of Judd's sculptures just below the level of consciousness. Every Judd sculpture resembles a non-specific auditory hallucination.

SUGAR COOKIE OC 94

As logotype developers know, color [like company paint] is the new psychotropic drug. Its purpose: systematically encode design or product information in the mind of consumers where it will "expire" like a memory. Unlike the past, when colors were expensive, durable luxury items whose names reflected the substances (azurite, lapis lazuli, cochineal, indigo, saffron, ultramarine) they were extracted from, today's luxury colors are synthetic, registered and very short. Trademarked color conditions reading patterns [as hallucinations] and triggers biochemical reactions ➜ emotions into moods. Practice is transformed into (programmed) pattern, just as lifestyle now precedes the life that lives it. In the future all products like books and furniture shall be deregulated and transmitted as moods or codes and these codes for beauty should be skin deep. No emotion should have to live and die like a disease in a glass box.

What are emotions we are about to have in a future already present? The era of emotions is over. One prefers a mood or mood predictor (mood rings, glo-balls, biofeedback devices, etc.), which in turn become logos for products, which in turn become product-emotions, which in turn become consumers (byproducts). In this way the consumer is always ahead of the feelings she is having, just as with Muzak, whose décor can minimize any room or elevator in the minute *before* one walks into it. The emotions one *almost* has just before and after purchasing something are among the most delicate species of emotions imaginable. They cannot be imagined. Such a state of pre-anticipation leads to relaxation.

This is a preface about the infrastructure of the audible and thus the emotions I am having and not having at the moment I am having them. The outlook is 2004, a muggy July 6–7 night [   ] when I have the air conditioning [   ] turned off and my apartment windows overlooking the Bowery [   ] are open to the street below [   ]. The diagrams for boredom are highly inaccurate. No one has yet come up with a trademark for things that are boring. What would a logo or index for boredom or low-level ambient artworks, what would such a thing look like? I think it would resemble a reptilian color that did not exist.

PREFACE (1978)

1

[Today]: This is a preface about time not passing and what it means to watch, really not watch a movie. I was in the FedEx office the other day waiting for a package to arrive and I realized that it means being indifferent to the things we are seeing at the moment we are seeing them. And by seeing I mean not [feeling] and not seeing. Only in that way is it possible to see the world repeat itself endlessly. As anyone who has waited for something to arrive can tell you, half an emotion is better than a whole one. The most beautiful emotions are half-hearted. Today I realized that I am [half] in love with my wife. As Herbert Blau noted: "An audience without a history is not an audience."

2

What is that thing known as difference? Like the ocean or a stop sign the film should be the most generic of surfaces imaginable. Because it is true, it should not be about seeing but about the erasure of things that were seen. The retina is boring and absorptive and a film should be no different. The eye scans backwards and forwards when reading. Only in that way can it repeat its own indifference and become all those things it cannot feel. This is known as boredom. In the most accurate movies nothing should be happening. Actors shall stop being actors. All events shall disappear into standardized non-events, like shopping. No emotions shall exist in order to be communicated. It is a well-known fact that shoppers in a supermarket rarely look closely at the things they are buying and this should be true of seeing films. Most of our physical pains, anxieties, and emotions are minor and disorganized like itches. As the authors of *Life and Its Replacement with a Dull Reflection of Itself* [1984] remark, "The observer can see less and less to complain about."

3

Because the retina is [weak], the [universe] tends to resemble nothing but itself.
[said]: The world is beautiful because it never stares back at you. Jacques Tati understood this perfectly when in *Playtime* all the interesting things that are not happening are not happening on the periphery of the shot. Most of us see [very little] and that is why the world is such a flat and beautiful place to linger in. Not looking at something is the highest compliment the eyes can pay to a landscape or a face. As anyone [who has been the subject of intense visual adoration] can tell you, staring at someone is the closest most of us will ever get to being a fly or falling in love. Like the bio-anthropology of everyday life [manners, cinema, acting, internet dating, check cashing, vitamin taking, the films of Maurice Pialat, the Discovery Channel, yoga, shopping], the ideal film would not create emotions but arrest them, ever more slowly, like fossils of the retina, and in that way estrange us from the drama of the lives we thought we were living. Vertov said that. An emotion that is waiting to happen is already dead. Not watching a movie is the closest thing to being an animal or reading a book whose pages have turned before we got there. A film should resemble the ambient space created by an airport, ID card photo, hotel, ATM machine, or all those things that happen to be around it. Not watching a movie is generally superior to watching one.

SECOND PREFACE (1986)

1

[Yesterday] I was reading a book called *Difference and Repetition* when my wife said: Emotions are the only way we have of making the world repeat itself. This is a preface about time standing still and what it means to not watch, really not watch a movie. I was in the FedEx office yesterday waiting for a package to arrive and I realized that it means to stop seeing the world repeat itself. In very beautiful movies, the film image becomes nothing more than an element in its own sequencing i.e. the sampling of a piece of furniture or a background color or wallpaper or perfume that [   ] occupied a room. Everything in a movie is redundant or everything that we fall in love with is mechanical. The film is as flagrant or lugubrious as a lawn chair. No one has to be an actor to die while speaking her lines.

2

What is that thing known as indifference? Enjoyment, like the face of someone we know, should be a species of dead or missing information. This is a preface about time not repeating like inexactitude and the reasons why so many words mean exactly the same thing. Laura Riding said that. Because the eye is the most relaxing thing we know, it tends to fall in love with only those things it cannot see. In this sense, the tracking number of the package I was waiting for resembles a film [I was not watching] and is meaningless in a distracted kind of way. The most beautiful faces (I have not seen) are the ones that resemble a cell phone or things that are dead. All faces like all films should be as generic, static and empty as possible. Emotions are the only way a human being has of repeating the same thing over and over.

3

What is that thing known as difference? Because the retina is boring and absorptive, I like an actor [who is no longer alive], a [tracking] number, or an obit [of a stranger]. Watching a film should constitute a [pattern] that "produces" highly generic content. The most beautiful emotions are outlines of emotions. I am very inattentive when I fall in love. As I tell my girlfriend who is now my wife, remembrance is a form of neglect. As patterns [of things that are non-existent], emotions are infrequent, dilatory or redundant. Having the same emotion twice is the most beautiful thing that a person can do to herself. Having an emotion once is a species of ugliness. That is why most artworks today are extremely ugly, why most faces are ugly until they become celebrities and we see them all the time, and why TV is the most beautiful medium around. A TV is made for staring at. Today I am half in love with my wife. That is why I love her so much.

4

[Today] [?] Something is [wrong] with this system [Roget]. One [kind] of thing can always be substituted by another [kind] of thing. 62

THIRD PREFACE (1998)

1

In Warhol's 3-minute screen tests, everyday people [who want to be stars] become faces and the faces become nothing more than a series of imperceptible twitches or blips on a blank surface. Facial information [input] translates into dull stereotypes. Dull stereotypes transmute occasionally into a system of stars or in Warhol's case, non-stars. The dullest stereotypes that exist today are name brands and generic celebrities. Despite the existence of brands, most shoppers buy w/o thinking or looking at the products they are buying. The same is true of faces. As psychologists have pointed out, staring at a face is one of the most unbearable things a human can do. Whenever I look at Andy Warhol's face I see a room named Delacroix.

2

Warhol understood that a film [every film is the same] is a branding device for the emotions and that the film is a medium wherein the spectator waits to see someone or something arbitrarily repeated. Warhol understood that this process could be systematized and mechanized and that *this*, not any arbitrary conjunction, is how we fall in love or not with people who we have never met. This might be termed a zero mass of events where the rules for genres fall apart. What is the look of an error before it occurs? Before I met my girlfriend, and I have told her this very often, I had fallen in love with her many times. The surface of love is porous and rigorous and illusionistic. The surface of Greta Garbo's face is the most beautiful template for the emotions because the surface is open and dead and arrives too late (for me to see). In much the same way, Warhol's faces are as blank and redundant and mathematical as faces in real life. They are stuck in moments of recurrence. They stare at things that are purely mechanical [the camera] or people who have not yet arrived and so cannot exchange their looks. They wait in celluloid for stardom to arrive. In these cases, it is difficult to tell the difference between a face whose expressiveness seems to trigger hallucinations and the involuntary, meaningless twitches of a face. Likewise it is difficult to distinguish between the drugged, anaphoric look of the smiling celebrity and the static, non-expressive head shot of the common criminal. As Helen Keller remarked: "Since I had no power of thought, I did not compare one mental state with another." What is the relation between an ordinary person and a celebrity? Repetition.

3

Warhol's head shots are quasi-legal documents that seek to regulate the passage of time and in that way the production of artworks, which is just another word for the emotions we probably won't have. In this sense they are like public forms of architecture. That is why people love [to go to] the movies [it is the simplest way of delaying one's emotions] from happening in order to make them appear [as if they are happening] later. Waiting is the greatest aphrodisiac known to humans and animals. Alcohol and drugs buffer the time zone between action and intentionality, and thus elongate the time between events and their interpretation (desired results). A box of chocolates, when ingested, has an amphetamine-like effect that people confuse with love. That is why I love to wait for my wife to show up in restaurants or laundromats or FedEx counters. She is always who she is even though the ambience of the room she is about to enter has changed in a thousand imperceptible ways before she arrives.

4

Warhol understood that waiting for a loved one was more interesting than actually falling in love and I have to agree. Of course most of the faces we fall in love with in real life never look at us. I have fallen out of love with Parker Posey quite a few times, in *The House of Yes*, in *Party Girl* and in *Basquiat*, and although each movie is different and unbearable to watch in its own way and in its own date/era, each time I fall in love is exactly the same as all the others. My wife looks like Parker Posey. As I was saying, our feelings are mainly repudiations of our feelings. Each of her faces is waiting like a fossil on my retina long before I arrive to interrupt this fact.

FOURTH PREFACE 2000

Poetry, film, novel, architecture and landscape are all management systems for distributing a set of related terms (RT). All generic templates [architecture, landscape, food, poetry, film, painting] possess the same underlying redundancy and exist for the same reason: to lose urgency, erase structural differences and suggest the most generalized of social anxieties as they pass over their surface where they appear to be something other than what they are. Happiness is mildly generic or it is not at all. Tolstoy said that. Waking should be like sleeping. Blandness is the new delivery model for all forms of entertainment. All the paths that our movements take end in repose and then awaken into something they are not.

That is why books we read today tend to resemble reality TV programs or shopping malls why television programs tend to resemble movies airports or parking garages why movies tend to resemble books we don't have time to read why design objects like flyswatters or blenders tend to resemble sculptures or insects or jewelry. Generic forms are much more useless than individual forms and are thus more highly prized. From them can be extracted all necessary i.e. redundant forms of information. Human memory resources are supremely limited and the most beautiful arrangements of reading material would be as immaterial, diffuse and ambient as the memory attached to them. As anyone who has read a book carelessly can tell you, forgetting a book is the most beautiful thing you can do to it. A very short book with lots of pictures can interrupt memory and the various modes of information glut and data blog that go with it.

FOURTH PREFACE REVISED 2000

What is the difference when a face is repeated? Like cracks to be repaired, all faces are unnecessarily redundant. Thus, it is possible to fall in love (again) and again and again with the things of the world. As any actor, hypnotized person, or ex-president will tell you, boredom is a form of perfection and everything that happens is ugly or inaccurate.

It would be preferable for a movie, if it were necessary to take place at all, to take place in the ambient corners of a room and in that way become the room in the same way that a novel becomes the place where the eye stops reading the words that are there. Film like reading should be about an unwilling suspension of disbelief. Film like life should not facilitate emotions but prevent them. For this reason, diagrams are useful. It is hard to experience an emotion that is a diagram but of course all our emotions are diagrams. Lars von Trier said that. That is the true nature of the cinema of attractions. Such a cinematic attractor would resemble a decrepit movie house like the Varsity Cinema I used to go to in Athens, Ohio, when I was growing up in the 70s and which was recently converted into a Taco Bell. A fast-food restaurant is the most beautiful kind of wallpaper the world knows how to create. The ideal movie is the most generic form of the thing we are no longer seeing anymore. Nothing could be more decorative than that. In this way, cinema might finally embrace all those inhuman patterns that are a part of our feelings: lifestyle, furniture, clichés, menus, the unread novel, the post office, corporate logos, the backs of books, pop music, soundtracks, bar codes. Seeing like reading should take place in a box or mildly controlled enclosure. The problem with intuitions is that they have too many flaws. The problem with most poems is that they have too many words. Instead of free texts, it would be nice to have extremely controlled vocabularies.

Highly generic, informal surface constraints (objects, organizations, practices, institutions) are the most beautiful ones.

Indexes of significant moments:

PUR

SMASHBOX	TROP-EX	FILTER 14	ETERNITY	VINEFIT LIP
OVERTURE	ADSENSE	STRENESSE	BOOKLAND	SMART TAG
SENSOTRONIC	LOGIXX	RESOLVE	T-57	LCW
PANTYTEC	NIXALITE	DUCO3044	ECLIPSE	MAXI CODE
FLEX DEVELOPMENT	VERY	ISS	PARASITE	ISOO
AGORIC SYSTEMS	NR2B	SANTOPRENE	FRIS	DYSPORT

Various Library Standards

DEDICATION to A WIFE:

11.07
2.21

FOUCAULT EPIGRAPH

There are no machines of freedom, by definition.

Index

Far from any idea of 'exhaustiveness' or the imposition of an 'order', this index aims merely to provide a few points of reference for some of the terms and concepts that occur in the essays collected here. Evidently, notions such as Writing, Subject, Text are developed constantly throughout the collection and can receive only token entries; proper names have been included solely when they stand for a textual practice important for that development.

Narrative *cont'd*
  temporality, 94, 98-9, 119

Obtuse ('third') meaning, 53, 54, 56-68
Obvious meaning, 52-3, 54, 55-6, 58, 62

Performative, 114 and *n*.1, 145-6
Pheno-/geno-text, 181, 182, 186, 187, 188
Photogenia, 23-4
Photograph, photographic image, 15-51
  and drawing, 17, 19 *n*., 25, 43, 44
  and film, 17, 18, 25, 45
  and painting, 24
  connotation procedures, 20-7
  connotation, status of codes of, 19, 28-31, 46-51
  denotation/connotation, 18-20, 34-7 *passim*
  denotation, status of photographic, 30, 32-3, 42-6
  in advertising, 32-51
  in press, 15-31, 40
  message without code, 17, 19, 36, 43, 45
  new space-time category, 44-5
  process of naturalization of message, 20, 26, 45-6, 50-1
  relations of linguistic matter to, 16, 25-7, 33-4, 37-41
  structures of linguistic understanding of, 28-9
Pose (photographic), 22

Quotation, 160, 177 and *n*.

Relay (image and linguistic matter), 38, 41
Representation, 64, 69-78, 182
  (*see also* Narrative)
Research, 197-8
Rhetoric, 49, 50 *n*.1, 83, 86, 96 *n*., 128, 162, 190
  of image, 18, 46-51
  signifying aspect of ideology, 49-50

Sentence, 82-4, 91, 165, 169
  (*see also* Narrative)
Sequence (in narrative), 101-4, 106, 128
  sequential analysis, 128-36
Signifiance, 12-13, 54, 65, 66 *n*., 126, 137, 141, 182, 183, 184, 185, 186, 207
Sollers, Philippe, 105 *n*., 157, 183 *n*., 187
Speech, 189
  and Law, 191-2
  and Other, 195
  irreversibility of, 190-2
  myth as, 165-6
  peaceable, 213-15
  (*see also* Writing)
Stereotype, 18, 165, 166, 168, 194-5, 198-9
Still, 65-8
Structural analysis, 37 *n*.1, 79-141 *passim*
Subject
  generalization of, 214
  in writing, 142, 145-6
  Lacanian topology of, 205
  linguistic analysis of, 105 *n*., 109, 112, 145
  status of in narrative analysis, 107-9

FOREWORD

This Foreword stands apart from the prefaces I have successively written for our book, in a period of twelve years. Its composition may be described as accumulative, progressing from an early personal statement through certain enlargements historically appropriate to its being of a more private character than the prefatory statements. It may be regarded as corresponding generally with the temporal expanse covered in the prefaces. The final portion of the Foreword is of late 1986—no arrangement for the book's publication being definitely in view at that time.

In the early 'thirties I began to feel a practical sense of urgency about something that had long troubled me. This was, that the use of words was in a bad way. The factor of urgency in my feelings was a product of accumulating awareness of the direct cause of the general state of word-use: it became plainer and plainer to me that the use of words was in a bad way because the knowledge of words was in a bad way. I committed myself to trying to make a new opening into the area of word-knowledge—the knowledge, that is, of what words mean. There is no conception of word-knowledge as a unity of words-knowledges. The characteristic conception of word-knowledge is, what this or that word means; there is no conception of language-knowledge as knowledge of the meanings of the words of a language in their interrelation as such. In my pursuit of my commitment, I did not meet an intellectually and morally companionate mind as to the things of language until I met Schuyler Brinckerhoff Jackson.

To the final stage of preparation of this book for possible publication, I had assumed that the preface I had written for it, as the completer of it for my husband and myself after he died, would be amply sufficient. What might need to be said preliminarily from the various personally and thematically relevant points of view seemed to have been said; and, also, as much of fortifying extension of the main matter seemed to have been included, in notes and supplementary articles, as could be accommodated in the book without overreaching

7

the boundaries of the subject (and, I hoped, those of the patience of the fully interested and serious readers). And yet there *is* more to say!

There seems to me to be need of a special candor [from] myself, as presiding authorially over the publishing eventualities on my and my husband's behalf, as to my view of what is here offered in it. I think that what is offered is a charter of human rights to the dignity of a speech of unlimited truth, and a declaration of linguistic independence from ideas of language that enslave the mind to other laws than those of its natural relation with its words. There is also in my attitude to the occasion of preparatory steps-taking towards the transforming of the book into a public actuality a very broad awareness (formed in long authorial experience) of the suspicious indifference with which writing that does not fall into any classification of kind but its own can be treated, especially when, being of its own kind, it is this with *sobriety*. Not only is this book of its own kind, by which I mean not that it is personally eccentric in its authorship, but that it is not adjusted in its "positions" to any others—mean that it has grown from the inside of its authors' hearts and minds to the public outside, and not the other way round (a course of growth that can never produce authentic internalities of feeling and thought): it is at the disadvantage, by the current criteria of "good" publicity-appeal, of being, as a work concerned with language, specifically *not* of a kind to come under the heading "Linguistics," or any heading of "semantic" reference (as "semiotics," "semiology"). "Linguistics" has a sub-heading, in letters inscribed in a manner intended to be visible only to writers on the subject of language, that reads: "Those who are not of us are against us, and will be as Naught. For we are the Synagogical All of The Modern Linguistic Communion."

Yet, despite our perceiving that our book had no place where to lay its head in the "linguistics"-dominated public world, we have not made Davidian effort in it to storm the linguistical strongholds, enter into battle royal against the Linguistical Armies with our homely personal forces. Readers may find that our not infrequent pausing to criticize features and aspects of professional, standard linguistics belies our repeated assurance that our book is not a polemical treatise. I urge them to try to adopt generally in their reading the attitude that they are people addressed on language as a subject concerning *them* primarily, in this book, as one involving reference to professional linguistics only because this exists to distract contemporary minds from their natural human orientations to language. We do not deal with linguistics other than as a distraction; in dealing with it, we deal with it as having that character. A distraction of its proportions cannot be proved to distract from, rather than promote, good aim of attention by being ignored.

There are happier matters to which reference is appropriate, in my parting words spoken as I look forward to sending this book forth into the public domain, than the conditions of language-interest obtaining in that domain; those conditions cannot be thought of as favorable to a hearty reception for the book—except as it might excite enough sensitivity to them to produce enough discomfort for an eventual tardy welcome.

I have had, in the years since my husband died, for protection in a solitude that includes dangers and deprivations, with its blessings, unfailingly adequate varieties of ministration from the neighbor-members of the citizenry of little Wabasso, and that of the environing county; this has remained constant, despite the gradually spreading conversion, since my husband and I came here to work, about thirty years ago, of the entire state of Florida into the site of a Fountain of Old Age, its waters of Easy-Life rising per ounce to out-of-sight cost—but those who flock here to drink tell themselves that the weather (poor, mere, mortality-reinforcing weather) comes free.

There are many, at varying distances, of precious name to me, to whom a path of devoted feeling stretches, broadened with gratitude for ready presence to me in the recent later years. I limit report of these to two. Both are of academic identity, but the identity of friend has reduced the other identity to an incidental fact for me, and for them also, in different measure and manner, according to differences of personal nature (the claims of academic identity being braved differently by different souls). The first of those that I name here is Robert S. Sproat, Professor of English at Boston University. He died on September 22, 1976. I came to understand through communication with him by letter and telephone (he "called" me about once a month, to keep us in closer than, just, written meeting) that Robert lived on three levels, moving from one to the other with no change in moral values, only changes in expectation of the kind of experience afforded at each. These were—as it seemed to me—the ordinary-life level, the intellectual-life level, and the level of the spiritually real. The last I think he visited as the place of most claim, but visited sparingly, as if to pay the respect to it of not making it a haunt of solitude. It seems to me that, when we talked by the grace of these telephone-calls, he put himself instantly at that level, as where we veritably met. I have felt given, ever, by him, the support of a fellow-believer in a best beyond qualifications. His was an extraordinary unity of values maintained across a division into different levels of value that he saw, sadly, as what "the world" did to one's life. But, while oppressed by the world's assumption of a right to have its way with one's life, he did not yield to it the right to nurse privately a hope of one's own. I am sad over his not having seen this book, which he wanted to see; I believe there is meeting between it and his hope. This is a reason to the fore, in my gladness in the book's becoming ready for public existence.

Of those who have been friend to me and to this book at far geographical distance, I shall name only one other (there are others, indeed). George S. Fraser, Professor of English at the University of Leicester, England, put an enthusiasm of faith in the importance of the book's coming into practical existence that contributed much to the speeding of it on its way to completion. Neither Robert Sproat nor George Fraser and I had any sight of each other. Friendship in both cases had to give recognition to differences in attitudes to things literary that cannot but amount to, in some senses, human differences. A few such sprung at times into prominence between George Fraser and myself, but I trust to the human affection that grew between us to prove us at one in the articles of linguistic faith to which this book subscribes that are, equally, articles of human faith.

I am hard put to it, in choosing persons of local identity to whom to pay gratitude's respect of special reference—neighbors, friends of the townlet and the county, who have been givers to me of the succor of loyal presence to me in my solitary work-perseverances. I shall choose just one, and let all the others be embraced in the identity of a company of kindness. I choose to name personally only a Negro man who became a friend of my husband and myself in years past, when he did work for us related to our fruit-growing and fruit-shipping activity. He made himself in a new way my friend after my husband died, seeking to exercise a protective care for needs of mine to which he might minister. He has a dramatic sense of himself. He can hardly read; but he is a lay preacher, keeps a Bible close at hand, exerts himself to propound Biblical and other maxims concerning the importance of at least trying to be perfect, and, in the first place, *making good one's word* (this, according to him, one's most important possession). *He* is not perfect. And I have discovered, pointing this out to him at times, that I too am a preacher!

Thinking on this man, and his reverent sense of the value of *words*, I am moved to point out how it is written in the Bible, as to exactitude: "For it must be precept on precept, line upon line, here a little, and there a little," (Isaiah), and how promise is given there of there being turned "to the people" a *pure language*. And it is said, further, that they will not "speak lies; neither shall a deceitful tongue be found in their mouth," (Zephaniah). And, later said, "For by thy words thou shalt be justified, and by thy words condemned"— and "Not that which goeth into the mouth defileth a man; but that which cometh out of the mouth, this defileth a man." I have said to Tom Herring, in preacher-manner, something of the following sort: "Good done does not show, it loses itself in the deed; what is done shines, not the doing, the doer." To which could be added, as to words: "What is proclaimed to be truth is only what is proclaimed to be truth. Words rightly spoken are true, but not because of a purpose to speak truth, only because of a purpose to speak rightly."

A most important mention of direct connection with my ability to carry the work of this book forward towards completion was the happy fortune of my being awarded a Fellowship of a year's duration by the John Simon Guggenheim Memorial Foundation. Through this support, physical and material burdens were lightened to an extent that brought completion within live view, besides allowing me to spare time and forces for other calls. There is also to be told that, beyond this happy relief, I have enjoyed interest on the Foundation's part in the book's progress towards completion, and its course towards publication.

But who could be found in this home region of mine, modest in its intellectual resources, capable of assisting me responsibly in the typing requirements and other needs of mine in this work—of giving the requisite accurate attention to the sustained course of intricate textual care? An at first unpromising trail of inquiry brought me eventually to young Susan Morris. It could not have been just her two years at the local Community College or her work-experience at the County library that made her equal to the handling of my manual script (found "difficult" by many), complicated by much correction and interpolation, at the typewriter, and working with me in perfect unison at checking points in the text and maintaining uniform three copies of the book. And there could be added other competences of hers, generously contributed to the total accomplishment. I think that perhaps my and the book's needs, and her store of capabilities, were made, if not in heaven, for each other, at least in Florida—which secretes an earthly providential beneficence the hiding-places of which have not all been dismantled by the destroying angels of civilization.

Finally, there is to include, within the bounty of Floridian donation, the hospitality and help extended to me by the Libraries of the University of Florida, for which I have personally to thank Dr. G. A. Harrer, Director, Dr. Laura V. Monti, Chairman, Department of Rare Books and Manuscripts, and Mr. Sherman L. Butler, Director of the Interlibrary-loans Department.

My relations with the University of Florida, of use of its library resources, became rather inactive as my work on our book moved towards completion, and my reading needs on its account were reduced. But even into these latest years I continue in friendly connection with its library quarters. The fact that I have for many years been a permanent resident of Florida has received some incidental attention in academic projects undertaken in the State for respect-paying to its affiliations with things literary. But what I have done of work of writing, and study for writing, in my Floridian home-place, has been done in a naturally discovered, naturally offered, freedom of privacy. What has been done here need make no trouble for anyone of concern with what to do about it as matter for report. It has been done as nobody's business except as it might be found to be everybody's business. My husband and I were let be—left alone to be, left alone to do—by the Floridian version of the nature of nature, which, I think, is, in its essential universality, to let be, and let do. I have clung to the protection of my acreage-portion of Floridian universality, keeping the

book in safe waiting, together with what I have been let do besides, for free-
dom for waiting long enough.

[An] end came to my having the support of Susan Morris in my labors. But
the support I had from her is built into what it enabled me to achieve. A
parting became necessary[:] in accepting it, I was left with the fact of the sup-
port, and the unalterable memory of it. The preacher-person has remained in
helping-hand association with me. I suffer many shortages in help, but there
is, to balance this, a varied consciousness of near and far concerned conscious-
ness of my predicaments of need. I am at peace with my circumstances.

     There is the death of George S. Fraser in 1980, to record. Our friendship
had lasted and became a close bond.

Strangely, in these whiles of seeming peace between my time of life and the
time of the world of human affairs, I have experienced assaults of literary and
personal malice that have no match, I believe, in vaunting liberties-taking with
innocent truth in our time. The touch of ill-will, even of betrayal, was not
new to me. But in these recent years I have been engulfed in a continuous
pandemonium of evil animadversions on my personal nature, my life, my
work. I have held my ground in this wild confusion of evil circumstance. Is
not hell, I have reflected, the swarm of everything indistinct that human beings
make of their language-powers? And is not the distinct, only the distinct, in
the shape of words brought out of thought into generous community of mind,
the only Friend?

     I have been caused weighty pain by the Enemy, the indistinct and its false
lying shapes of distinctness, as it has sway in the world of intellectual (literary,
scholarly) life. The weight of the pain of personal injury has kept dissolving
itself in the pain of consciousness of wide-spread falsifications of the human
state enveloping it in the lie of its being itself a pandemonium in which peace
and pleasure can only be achieved by techniques of treating it as a painfully
absurd state—in which peace and pleasure can be no more than contrived
stupefactions. On what I count as saving surety, in my sense of spreading pan-
demonium, for the prevailing of an unfailing Distinct over a ruinous Indistinct
(a continuous lexicon of novelties in meaninglessness), this book has a central
position. It presents the scene of the human mind of now as a place of choice,
still, between a hellish ease of speech-making thought as easy as no-thought
and heaven-like difficulty of thought executed with an earthly ease of speech
the mind can love.

                                                              1986
                                                    Wabasso, Florida

PEA (phenyl ethylamine) → sex

The activity of lovemaking, like film or reading, should function in the same way as a hotel room, fringe area, e-mail address, train ticket, parking garage, or light manufacturing building converted into luxury condo or nightclub. A movie is merely the sum of information the movie contains and one never really wants to enjoy information too much. Ditto a lover. All transformations between warehouse and loft, clubhouse and fairway, poem and restaurant shall be rendered invisible or subject to unknown feelings. A film should be as imperceptible as an aphrodisiac. For this reason, it is a very bad idea to fall in love while renting a DVD. A movie of an empty parking lot on a Sunday afternoon would be a very beautiful movie because it resembles a very long bout of foreplay or an unplayable lie.

Like a sudden spike in internet traffic, film should be extremely collective. Like the instrumental non-collective mob at Macy's, film should create a structure-less event or a set of standardized behavior patterns that could slip into a pattern of laziness and redundancy. A film is a form that is not a form in the same way that TV and golf courses are. The best non-pornographic sport to watch on TV is a golfing "event" because it is the closet thing one can come to watching a landscape doing nothing and becoming something routine and non-functional. Debord was wrong. Golf is not about spectacle it is about the absence or total absorption of spectacle into a definition set. What is the *derive* but erasure: the "bland re-surfacing through the lack-luster changes of an environment's information levels."

CONCLUSION (REV 2002)

Thus the most generic landscape is the *least* forgettable and today that landscape is the airport, shopping mall or golf course, where nature is standardized and converted into a data container or Document Type Definition. One of the hardest things to get nostalgic over is a definition for a golf course. A golf course is essentially a template for the living room's carpeted expanses, its controlled sight lines and its standardized exercise and equipment routines. On a golf course, everything is already labeled. Tee markers are laid out and "calculated." Distances are computed via brochure-sized maps. Individual difficulty [absurdity] is standardized and handicapped. Depths (vistas) are converted into playable surfaces with precise yardages marked by flags. There is nothing so civilized and unrhetorical as the recursive rhythms of a golf game. Everyone knows it is very very difficult to have any memories—good or bad—while golfing. Such feelings are systemic.

In the future, the most beautiful golf courses will be those that allow the players to play sitting down or while reading a book or painting a painting or making love. The old shopping malls are now dying. Pretty soon people will start getting nostalgic about them and that will be too bad. Golfing is the new shopping. That is why even though I am/was married I still frequent on-line dating services. The problem with history is that it has already taken place.

ACKNOWLEDGMENTS

The author would like to thank

Clare Churchouse

for cover design work, lettering and much much more

Charles Bernstein

Danielle Aubert and Ellen Quinn

for generous design support

Mitchy Uno, who designed, directed,
and laid out pages

Ann Albright, Suzanna Tamminen, Leslie Starr, Stephanie Elliot

@wesleyan.edu, Peter Fong at UPNE,

Gordon Tapper and Jonathan Flatley for reading

my mother for 紮\饌舻

and much more, the Pickwick Arms Hotel

Andrei [Timofeevich] Bolotov's editors, Maya Lin

Ethan Bumas, Jo Bruno at New Jersey City University

Kenny Goldsmith, Warren Liu, Dorothy Wang, and Lyn Hejinian

the editors:

Conjunctions, No: A Journal of the Arts, The Capilano Review,
and *XCP: Cross Cultural Poetics*

and Ahn

SEVENTH PREFACE 2003

As any architect like Rem Koolhaas or Frank Gehry can tell you, there is nothing more egotistical than a very large structure that has the word sculpture or information imprinted on it. It would be nice to enter a building and not know one was [   ] in a building. Buildings without architects, poems without authors and films without directors are the most beautiful things imaginable. They can hardly be imagined.

The brain is the great averager. For this reason, it knows how to relax. Literature should be an elaboration of relaxation formats, sensory deprivation and disordered or arbitrary input that has been channeled or reduced to non-stimuli. Thus, after relaxation or sensory deprivation is induced the following forms might be hallucinated because they are utterly redundant. The brain is the great averager. It knows how to program its own boredom. Explanations have to stop somewhere. Wittgenstein said that. Absolutely perfect symmetry can answer every question with yes or no. The following chart occurs where explanations are rendered generic, redundant and plastic. Amorphousness is the new symmetry. Gaps and temporal overlaps rather than voids dominate. Robert Smithson was wrong. It is culture not nature that loves a vacuum or outline of itself. Hence, a non-hierarchical flow chart outlines the various states of cultural category disorder (flow) in the next decade. The chart is read bidirectionally:

APPENDIX

SLOW	ITERATIVE/FUZZY	FLAT
logos		
ticket stubs		
fast food	customized	
cash register receipts		
drug prescriptions		
bar codes		species of geometric
forms		

SLOWER	RECURSIVE/UNFINISHED	FLATTER
golf courses		
shopping malls		
airports	branded	
hotels		species of objective forms
parking lots		

SLO/SOFT	INFINITELY LOOPED/FORMAL	ULTRA FLAT
blindfolded paintings		
computer-generated novels		
amateur "puzzles"		
memory-less memoirs	under sanctioned/contextualized	
faux film		
Reality Poetry		
Dullness Tropes (photo)		
DIY Incompetence		
Reality Poetry (non-practice based)		species of symbolic forms

EIGHTH PREFACE 2004

[Today] architecture, film, poetry etc. should aspire to objective and geometric forms rather than symbolic forms embedded in Naturalism, Completeness, Realism, Depth and Identity. Poetry is Conventional. For that reason it is not conventionally perceived as symmetrical with logos or parking lots or New Age crystals, which are regarded as prefabricated surfaces, conduits, or resonances, respectively. A poem, film, novel or painting is an asymmetrical, aperiodic, slow repeater and by that method achieves complementary arrangements with the world at large. Typically, the poem like the film or building repeats things that are external to it. Repetition or redundancy becomes the predominant mode of dissymmetry, and the matching processes that this engenders in the brain are deemed aesthetic/pleasurable. The problem is that most poems and films give off too much pleasure. They are not redundant or boring or ambient or generic or flat or iterative or fringe-like or soft enough. Asymmetry suggests diversion [recreation] from the two principal routines of modern life, namely shopping and watching TV, which are the most highly symmetric formations today.

Culture tends to repeat itself ad nauseum and this repetition takes numerous forms, some of which are more boring than others: rotational symmetry, planar symmetry, glide reflections, inversion, and translation. In most eastern and nomadic cultures, life within the tent is dominated by homemade things covered with geometric designs whereas in western cities, surroundings are geometric and household objects such as plants, pets, artworks, and even utensils are designed to have shapes that are perceived to be as natural, biomorphic and asymmetrical as function will allow. Patterns do not communicate emotions, they absorb them. Thus, Antiochus in Racine's *Bérénice*: "Dans l'Orient désert, quel devint mon ennui!"

The perfect poem or film would be completely symmetrical, geometric and objective. Also: boring and ambient and not very insistent. Events like people in crowds should be as sedated as possible. Events should disperse into their own events. Each cinematic image would be as similar as possible to the one that immediately preceded it. What is an image but a set of events that cannot be written about. I had a hallucination or I watched a movie where nothing was happening. Only in that way can a film a landscape a face become a tracking system whose purpose is to register frequency or probability rather than communicate any emotional content. After one sees a movie, one leaves the theatre. One never wants to have to see a movie to enjoy it. My girlfriend looks like Greta Garbo. In the real world, nobody has to be an actor to remember her lines. Nothing that is generic needs something specific to reinforce it.

The author would also like to thank the following individuals and institutions for help in the production of this book:

Maureen Sarro, Colby Bird, Friedrich Petzel Gallery, Jane Rolo, Book Works, Angie Hogan, University of Virginia Press, Farrar Strauss and Giroux, Timothy Bewes, Verso Books, Chris Johanson, Jasmine Levitt, Deitch Projects, TVRT Press, the estate of Kathy Acker, Julian Rothenstein, Redstone Press, Pattie McCarthy, Beautiful Swimmer Press, Geoffrey Young, The Figures, Clayton Eshleman, Caterpillar, Wesleyan University Press, Unionbay, Seattle Pacific Industries, Jess, Kimura Hiroshi, Zush, A.A. Bronson, Printed Matter, Yvon Lambert, Adam Kalkin, Batsford Books, Matias Viegener, Emily Post, Lester Freundlich, the MTA, Donna Dennison, Bedford St. Martin's, Jonathan Cape, Marianne Boesky Gallery, Gary Sullivan, Jack Kimball, Faux Press, The Joy of Cooking (1975), Plume Editions, Tibor de Nagy Gallery, Penguin Books, Gerhard Theewen, Salon Verlag, Vivienne Westwood, Maison Martin Margiela, Allan Sams, Anova Books, Walter Mortensen, Perceval Press, Tim Brock, National Towelette Company, Inc., Rachel Carron, WD-50, Manuel Brito.

DIRECT SALES

10 FORMATS FOR

"BOOK YOU ARE READING"
EDITION SIZE: 2000.
$22.95 PBK

EDITION SIZE: 150.
$50 HARDCOVER IN ORANGE BUCKRAM
LIBRARY BINDING WITH BLACK STAMPING

ED. WITH HAND-NUMBERED BLURB
EDITION SIZE: 10. $11.07
AVAILABLE BY EMAILING THE AUTHOR VIA THE PRESS

POETRY MOVIE, *DISCO M FIGURE*
A CD WITH 100-MINUTE SELECTION OF POETIC WALLPAPER
EDITION SIZE: 50. SUITABLE FOR PROJECTION $750
ALSO AVAILABLE FREE AT
HTTP://WRITING.UPENN.EDU/PENNSOUND/X/LIN.HTML

ALSO AVAILABLE AS A PLEXIGLAS VIDEO INSTALLATION,
WITH 3 LCD MONITORS AND PROCESSOR
EDITION SIZE: 3. $12,000

A LETTER-PRESS BLURB SHEET
EDITION SIZE: 42. $211.01

A LETTER-PRESS BROADSIDE FRONT-BACK-COVER REPRODUCTION
EDITION SIZE: 47. $604.00

CHAPTER 1 IS AVAILABLE AS *HOME + LIFESTYLE*,
A DINING = LITERACY PLACEMAT
IN THERMAL-PRINTED PLASTIC. IN A CHOICE OF 7 NEON COLORS
EDITION SIZE: 400. $54

A LULU EDITION. 2004. EDITION SIZE: 50. $12.95
[OUT OF PRINT]

[TRADITIONAL REPRINT ED. TBA]

FIG 1   FIG 2   FIG 3   FIG 4.

A Field Guide to American Cinema

7CNTRLD B

]ASSEMBLY

COMMON

S    L ISP

DOCUMMEN

T FUNCTION

X3.226-199

4 (R1999)

[VOCABULA

META DATA S-XPRESSIO NS

DISJOINT UN ION

png_create_write_struct
png_get_signature
png_read_row
png_set_invalid

SYNONYM

RINGS OBJECT ID™

T

GObject
NAMESPACE

Some said her unpredictability

That summer

I constructed

a wind measurement machine

It read "It was like paint." Or said:

It said: it generated it waved its wand it bruised face it inebriated it inserted a needle with

the notes were tobacco like

it

"I strung parts with piano" wire.

follicle-stimulating hormone [FSH]

Some said going out.

Some That Pres ident tied up

some of them plaintive and horny

That I was in love with my girlfriend's

music grid (when I get)

the wire part, the wood-leaf variant A-78903

which resembles

movie (4   millimeter)

Tattoo That rese

                                                              Some of th   em

        irons That summer: t   ann   ing th   msel   ves fu   cking.

                                                    I came

                                        Because   I

a   miniature

mbled golfc   ourse

were practici   ng   sho   ·   rt

in

had not fallen in love　;　None of them remembers what　age I

It　rained a lot　-　It was shitty to be child-less　　　"　"　"

And their friends

who said they were   ,   I was dropping   '   It was "

bead lamp   :   And   . They were engaged (   )

Some of them were   ,   Not about ; hassling   ;   My father   ;   [Mobile]

They were eating in   ?   )   302.0
Chinatown

They saw   each other occasionally

None of them   they screwed a fake console

over the ATM   machines

or fucking him twice

someone was putting

inside a can onfire

and some of them when they got there

\

tried to put it out

the men had used

They counted 1–10

they he the and the morning

round [   ] dope

They were sewing firing

caps into

lining the suitcases

And shitting around   That spring They came up with slogans. Blandness was their

entertainment. The horses push thru

P = Some were looking at it [hotel room/airport/v-neck] like sand = cake and imploring

They were talking about leather
seats in

the Lexus

PART II

looking kissing voting

Peter was

dancing with his shirt around his waist, which he tied to them

they had something

like pollen on their teeth,

I sat

It was 1969. They owned.

In

a Pinto.

the door

It was summer

you were

his second roommate

Peter was dancing

that summer

Someone   Hitting

my leg
talking about the parking garage with 14 people dead

1

of them remembers

the building on top didn't collapse

that she

registered

to take C++

she was barely five feet tall.

etc. etc.

had miscarriage

Some said moving the car

some said in the sink that morning

The picnic table

littered with Dove Bars, etc. etc. wiring casings etc. etc.

It was 1987. There was dust from the NE tower

It was not

February. They did not remember moving the car or which way it was parked.

They bit

fk 3

fo 45

2 mins 56 secs
4 mins 17 secs

each other occasionally during intercourse

It was not February.

They did not talk much when they met the third time.

They were listening to the Mekons

In the morning they watched TV about a bomb going through

a parking garage

someone's _____

We fell off One of us graduated

While One of them had something personable.

Some were back school or hanging around waiting

making t-shirts in their mother's basement

While her

her father was smoking we were white

we were black and the car was white

Courtesy limo was an artichoke vinaigrette salad

They had sex in a movie theatre.

Latino Because They hated me

They had thought about the Republic that way

She was

36

17

I was reading Plato all summer they were visiting

strip club

I am

not

with

Some of them

inserted cigarettes inside the lining they were smoking

a white Pinto, with a bomb under the tire

Some that

Poetry Reading

Fruits that lose their smell when burned

(remote & ephemeral)

L: Cinema should aspire to the most taciturn forms of expression such as greeting cards, photographs of outer space, video monitors turned off, slightly incandescent lightbulbs, automobile windshields at night, billboards, cheap but glossy high-quality reproductions (of photos or paintings), banners, employment manuals, flags. The best movies would consist only of words or letters. Unlike images, letters never change.

R: A book should reflect the symbols that pass before it before they become emotions. In the ugliest of books, all emotions become the symbols of things that they are not. Like the Pantone color chart, the beautiful book is a diagram of "historical inexactitude" which reflects (by turning) something "not there." What is "not there" is opposed to what appears in a mirror. It should never be necessary to turn a page when reading. The page should turn before you got there. This is known as history.

END

polio   implants   Wal-Mart

WEDGE   SPL   SINGLE

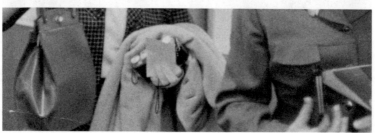

exit]

ABOUT the AUTHOR

Tan Lin has published three books of poetry: *Lotion Bullwhip Giraffe* (Sun & Moon Press, 1996), *BlipSoak01* (Atelos, 2003), and *Heath, plagiarism/outsource* (Zasterle, 2007). He is a professor of English and creative writing at New Jersey City University.

(continued from page 123)

this idea: contestants engage in the "work" of losing weight, being made over, marrying a millionaire, or undergoing plastic surgery. Here, the fantasy of work supplants work itself. Or does it? One person's free time is another person's profit. A commodified life has the potential to make money because commodification can be unpleasant [your identity = somebody else's intellectual property], as witness the machinations of Omarosa, who claims to be "just playing the game" but who the audience perceives as evil. Why is she behaving as she does? Because she is on TV. Is she being coached? Of course. Was she specifically cast for her role as prime-time bitch? Of course. The fact that the apparent flatness of the game-show conceit generates something "unpredictable" is decisive for the viewer, who is riveted by a celebrity void at the center of the network's programming: who is Omarosa and why is she doing the things she does? Evil and love [and now reality TV] give off the appearance of being unpredictable motivational voids at the center of the network's programming; hence their presence on daytime soaps and prime-time dramas. The networks are well aware that subjective events like emotions are relatively easy to control and standardize in a viewer, as the TV camera in the boardroom reveals. Of course, the people on shows like *The Apprentice* are subjective events destined for a single viewing season, but it's not their personalities that matter, it's the void at the center of the viewer's experiences that counts. As most network executives can tell you, the mediation of a life on television—like an emotion—is short-lived, and the reality behind the play reality is hardly a luxury because it is about transforming something into nothing: each minute of the viewer's unpaid leisure time becomes work time in order that we may resemble quasi-celebrities like ourselves.